YOUNG MAN ·WITH· CAMERA

BY
EMIL SHER

PICTURES BY DAVID WYMAN

Scholastic Canada Ltd.
Toronto New York London Auckland Sydney
Mexico City New Delhi Hong Kong Buenos Aires

Scholastic Canada Ltd.
604 King Street West, Toronto, Ontario M5V 1E1, Canada

Scholastic Inc.
557 Broadway, New York, NY 10012, USA

Scholastic Australia Pty Limited
PO Box 579, Gosford, NSW 2250, Australia

Scholastic New Zealand Limited
Private Bag 94407, Botany, Manukau 2163, New Zealand

Scholastic Children's Books
Euston House, 24 Eversholt Street, London NW1 1DB, UK

www.scholastic.ca

Library and Archives Canada Cataloguing in Publication
Sher, Emil, 1959-, author
Young man with camera / by Emil Sher ; photography
by David Wyman.
Previously published: New York, NY: Arthur A. Levine
Books, an imprint of Scholastic Inc., 2015.
ISBN 978-1-4431-0401-2 (softcover)
I. Wyman, David M., 1948-, photographer II. Title.
PS8587.H38535Y68 2017   jC813'.54   C2017-901519-2

*The author gratefully acknowledges the support of the Ontario Arts Council and the City of
Toronto through the Toronto Arts Council.*

ONTARIO ARTS COUNCIL
CONSEIL DES ARTS DE L'ONTARIO
an Ontario government agency
un organisme du gouvernement de l'Ontario

TORONTO
ARTS
COUNCIL

FUNDED BY
THE CITY OF
TORONTO

CELEBRATING **40** YEARS

RECYCLED
Paper made from
recycled material
FSC
www.fsc.org   FSC® C103567

For Kathryn

Praise for
Young Man with Camera

★ Winner of the Vine Award for Canadian Jewish Literature

★ Shortlisted for the Governor General's Award
for Children's Literature — Text

★ Honour Book, Canadian Library Association
Book of the Year for Children Award

★ Shortlisted for the Ruth and Sylvia Schwartz Award

★ Shortlisted for the Amy Mathers Teen Book Award

★ Shortlisted for the Red Maple Award

★ Shortlisted for the Snow Willow Award

★ *VOYA* magazine Perfect Ten selection

"This is a novel about the beauty that lies within, the darkness that comes
from without, and the grace and nobility of a boy who sees it all through
his lens. You will grow larger for having read this book."
— Gary D. Schmidt, Newbery Honor–winning author of
The Wednesday Wars and *Orbiting Jupiter*

"A brilliantly original voice and a gut-twisting story come together
for a dazzling jewel of a book. Truly outstanding."
— Kevin Brooks, author of *Candy* and *The Bunker Diary*

"One of the few books for this generation that will stick with them into adulthood."
— *The Globe and Mail*

"[Emil Sher's] masterful use of beautifully evocative language creates vivid pictures in the mind of the reader, which are complemented by David Wyman's unembellished yet achingly expressive photographs."
— *Quill & Quire*

"The hope here lies . . . in T—'s photographs, stark, expressive black-and-white portraits that appear interspersed with the text and add depth . . . Bleak yet life-affirming."
— *Kirkus*

"A gripping look at bullying, its outcomes, and the reasons why some kids can't 'just say no'. . . . Should be a staple in English classes."
— *School Library Journal*

"Every once in a while you read a book that really sticks with you. You can't get a character or a plot out of your head and think about the book for days. *Young Man with Camera*, by Emil Sher, is one of those books."
— *CM: Canadian Review of Materials*

This is not a fire hydrant.

It's a photograph of a fire hydrant. And the truth is, a hydrant isn't always a hydrant.

Sometimes it's a perch.

I stood on my perch to take a picture of Ruby. Ruby is Mr. Lam's daughter. Mr. Lam is the owner of McCreary's Corner Store, which is a lie, since the store is in the middle of the block and should be called McCreary's Nowhere-Near-the-Corner Store. Most of the time, when Mr. Lam is inside, scanning the aisles for shoplifters, Ruby is outside, drawing pictures with chalk.

Once Ruby knows what she's going to draw, it's a short walk between *decide* and *done*. I took a bunch of photographs to add to my *Sidewalk Series*. That's what I call my pictures of Ruby and her sidewalk drawings. Ruby crouched on one spot. Ruby blowing chalk dust. Ruby carefully tracing a line.

She was adding another leaf to a beanstalk (no Jack) and I was on my perch when I heard them. Ryan, Jared, and Med are a thunder-and-black-cloud combination. You know a storm is coming before a drop of rain hits the ground.

Hey, mutant!

Ryan raised his hands, as if he was under arrest.

Don't shoot!

He grinned. Then Med and Jared grinned, as if they hadn't heard the line a thousand times before.

What're you doing up there?

All three of them surrounded the hydrant.

You waiting to put out a fire? Ryan asked.

I didn't say anything. Whatever I said would be twisted and sharpened and flung right back at me.

Ruby was watching from one corner of her eye. She was trying not to look, but I could see it was a busy corner.

You don't look like much of a hydrant.

Ryan looked at Jared and Med.

Does the dipstick look like a fire hydrant to you?

Jared and Med shook their heads. Ryan took a swing at my ankles. I fell to the ground and ended up on my knees, next to Ruby's beanstalk.

Ryan walked over and pulled a matchbook out of his pocket. He lit a match. He pinched it between his fingers, then held the flame about an inch away from my face.

I blew out the match and extinguished his grin.

Then he smiled again, slowly. **So you *do* think you're a hydrant.**

I stared at a beanstalk leaf. I didn't know what he would do next. Hot one minute, cold the next. Ryan is like the weather, only none of his clouds has a silver lining.

He turned to Jared and Med and pretended to be concerned. **He's too dry for a hydrant**, he said. He took his water bottle out of his backpack. **We're here to help.**

The bottle was half-filled. Then it wasn't.

That's better.

I felt the water run down my back. My shirt got heavy and damp. I covered my camera with both hands.

Ryan motioned to Jared and Med with a small nod. They nodded back. By the time Med was finished, my pants were soaked. Ryan orders, they obey. That's why I call them Joined at the Hip. I've been their target practice since kindergarten. Most days I'm more target than practice.

Jared had just taken the cap off his water bottle when I saw Ruby's beanstalk getting dark-spot wet. I knocked the bottle out of his hands. The bottle — and most of the water — landed on Ryan's feet.

Ryan yanked me up by the collar and started to twist my shirt. Then he stopped. Mr. Lam had stepped out of his store.

Are you okay? Ryan asked me. He put his hand on my shoulder. Ryan the sugar-coated stone. You can't see what's inside.

Did you see what happened? he asked Mr. Lam. Every word was sweet and smooth. **We got here and found him like this.**

Mr. Lam didn't answer. He stared at Ruby: *I want you inside.* He stared at Ryan: *I want you out of here.* Then he stared at waterlogged me: *What the heck?*

Ruby poked her head out from behind her father. Mr. Lam waited for Joined at the Hip to finish pretending to care about me. They tugged at my soaked shirt. Patted my soaked back. Adjusted my camera strap. They took their sweet time. Ryan tried to make it sweeter until Mr. Lam grunted. Mr. Lam grunts a lot, like my father. They both speak Grunt.

Ryan walked away. Med and Jared followed. Mr. Lam led Ruby back into the store.

I was the only one left. Me and a bruised beanstalk. Some water from Jared's bottle had spilled as it spun out of his hand. I grabbed the chalk that Ruby had left on the sidewalk and tried to repair the damage.

I was halfway up the stalk before I noticed Ruby poking her head out of the door. She gave me a smile so small I could have put it in my pocket and forgotten it was there. She opened the door wider and wider and wider.

I stepped inside. Ruby disappeared.

Someone named McCreary must have owned McCreary's Middle-of-the-Block Store a thousand years ago, but Mr. Lam never changed the name. Nothing ever changes at McCreary's, especially Mr. Lam's attitude. He hates kids, which is a problem because the place is wall-to-wall kids at lunchtime and after school. Joined at the Hip steal chips and chocolate bars from him, but they're always polite, so he never suspects them. He thinks other kids are stealing from him instead and yells *Pay, pay!* at all of us. Some kids call him Mr. Paypay behind his back. Other kids don't wait for him to turn around.

As I stood by the door, Mr. Lam kept watching me, even though I had never stolen anything. That's what happens when you have a different-looking face. People look at you differently. Most of my face is normal but "most" isn't enough to stop all the stares. Once abnormal moves into the neighborhood — scars up my neck and across one cheek — normal might as well pack up and leave.

I'm glad I wasn't wearing my hoodie that day or Mr. Lam's dirty looks would have been dirtier. He thinks anyone who wears a hoodie is up to no good. Mine has a big-as-a-plate camera lens printed on the back. I wear it on days when I get tired of stares. A hoodie is a scar's best friend.

Ruby showed up from the back of the store holding a paper towel roll. She gave it to me. I said, **Thank you.** She didn't say anything. I had a feeling her shyness had swallowed her smile. You can't tell she's shy in any of my *Sidewalk* photographs.

I dried myself off with the paper towels, then bought some candy as a way of saying thanks to Ruby for opening the door.

Mr. Lam stared at me as I left. If he was waiting for the truth about what had happened with Ryan, he would have a long wait. The truth is like our kitchen wall. It looks yellow. It is yellow. But there's more than one yellow. Truth, like yellow, comes in a thousand different shades.

By the time I got to the park, I was as dry as the empty wading pool where I stood and waited for Sean. It's the same wading pool where Sean and I once sat as two-year-olds in four inches of water. It's the same park where Sean brought Watson when he was just a few pounds of sock-eating mischief. It's where we kick around a soccer ball because soccer is about the only game we can play without getting bruised or beaned. All you need is a foot, and Sean and I each have two.

But we don't have flow. That's what our gym teacher, Mr. Ramshaw, calls it. "Flow" is another way of saying *You're a good athlete*. Mr. Ramshaw doesn't care what you're like as a person as long as you have flow. If you eat babies but are good at basketball, he wants you on his team. Ryan, Jared, and Med all have flow. So do Owen, Mitchell, and Lee, who make up the rest of Ryan's crew. If you ask me, photographers can also have flow, but Mr. Ramshaw's "flow" doesn't flow past the gym floor.

I knew Sean had arrived when I felt Watson chewing a mouthful of my pants. Shredding pants and treating shoelaces like spaghetti is Watson's way of showing affection.

No, Watson!

Sean yells *No, Watson!* so often Watson must think it's his full name. He said it again as he pulled Watson off my leg with one hand, then tossed a soccer ball with the other. Watson ran after it, and Sean ran after Watson.

I once told Sean I was going to get a dog named Sherlock because every Watson needs a Sherlock, and he said, *Every Sherlock needs a Watson*. Then we made a list of all the people who needed each other, like Han Solo and Chewbacca, or Batman and Robin. I need Sean because he knows exactly when to speak Silence. After my run-in with Joined at the Hip, a back-and-forth ball was the only kind of conversation I wanted to have. Sean kicked the ball to me, and we spent ten minutes knocking it around until Sean said, **Halftime**, and pointed to his backpack.

We sat by a tree with muffins Sean's mother had made. In the Book of Parents, Sean's mother is mentioned in two chapters: Best Tailor and Worst Cook. Her muffins look like muffins, but once you take a bite, you realize they're not related to any other muffin ever and must have been adopted. I nibbled on mine. Sean nibbled on his. Five nibbles later we tossed the muffins to Watson, who practically inhaled them.

Sean handed me another muffin.

What am I supposed to do with this?

He shrugged. **I can't take it home.**

Give it to Watson.

He shook his head. **Too many mystery muffins aren't good for him.**

I nodded and stuffed the muffin into my backpack.

Sean took out a container of watery, homemade pudding and stuck a straw into it.

Pudding is supposed to be eaten with a spoon, I said.

History books are packed with people who did things

differently, he said between straw-sucking sips. **First they were laughed at, but they had the last laugh. They finally got the glory they deserved.**

I thought about history books that don't exist, filled with people who were laughed at and then made a quick getaway because they couldn't stand the laughing. By the time they found glory no one was around to write about it.

History books are like photographs in that way. You only get part of the picture. In *Beanstalk* all you see is Ruby adding a leaf. You can't see Joined at the Hip, who are out of the frame but about to make trouble.

I told Sean how they had ruined my day and Ruby's drawing. **It sucks when kids like Ruby end up getting grazed by Ryan.**

Sean nodded as he took a long sip of his pudding and stared ahead. I tried to see what he was staring at. All I saw was an old man feeding pigeons and a woman unpacking a picnic on a blanket, laughing while a man poured chips into a bowl.

We need poison to deal with him, Sean said. **Or cement shoes.**

Sean devours mystery novels, so he knows all about revenge.

You put a person's feet in wet cement and wait for the cement to dry and then you dump him into a river.

He tossed the pudding container into his backpack and started chewing on his straw.

Or you hide the body in a construction site and wait for the construction workers to pour wet cement. Then the body is inside the walls forever and you'll never get caught.

I shook my head. **I don't want to use poison or hide bodies in walls. I just want Joined at the Hip to disappear. Not murder. More like magic.**

Joined at the Hip has tormented me for years. It started small (dipping my hand in pumpkin guts in grade one). Gym meant shorts yanked to my ankles (grade five). Lunch money was quietly extorted. Arms were twisted but never bruised. Last year they blocked and broke a toilet and I was blamed for the damage. I've tried talking to my parents, but they're like all the teachers — in awe of Ryan. When he pours on the charm he never needs a refill.

Sean started making different designs with his straw. He does that when he's thinking. Sometimes he gets so caught up in what he's making that he forgets where he is, lost in his own world. Sometimes I think we're in the same boat but in different worlds, and the boat we share travels back and forth between worlds.

Magic wouldn't work, T— Sean said. **At a magic show, the bunny disappears, but at the end, the bunny is back. We don't want the bunny to come back.**

Only a couple of kids in school call me T—. Most don't bother calling me anything. The ones that do call me things you would never say at a dinner table unless you wanted to be grounded for six years. I don't like to write out my name because I know someone will come along and twist a normal name into something not-normal.

Sean and I spoke Silence for another five minutes. I kept thinking about end-of-show bunnies.

Want to take some pictures? Sean said at last.

He grinned at me. Something happens when I hold a camera. It's like the camera holds me. My photographs will outlast Ryan.

Did you show her your pictures yet? Sean asked between clicks.

The *her* was Ms. Karamath, the new librarian at our school. She had introduced herself as *fair but firm. Patient, but not a pushover.* And *curious.* That's what she said when Sean told her about my photographs — that she was curious and *anxious to see them.* Ever since then Sean had been bugging me to show them to her.

I want to make sure I choose the right ones, I told Sean.

You promised you'd bring them in.

I nodded. **I haven't been to the Vault in a couple of days.** I couldn't wait to get back.

One more, he said.

Sean wrapped an arm around Watson, and Watson — a dog who never sits still, a dog with ADD — looked like he didn't want to be anywhere else.

Until he saw a squirrel in the distance.

No, Watson!

Watson bolted across the park. Sean was about to chase after him, but then he stopped. His eyes turned to stones that would never shine no matter how much you polished them. I turned to see what he was looking at.

Jared was walking across the park, holding the hand of a little girl who looked exactly like him. Only this version of Jared had her hair in pigtails and wore a banana-yellow dress.

Olive, I said. His little sister.

I looked at Jared to see if he was looking at us. He eyeballed us for a second, just long enough for a quick sneer, then he turned away.

The sneer wasn't even real, as lame as the fake teeth you wear at Halloween.

He looks different.

He looks the same, Sean said.

Jared dropped Olive's hand. She looked confused and tugged at one hand, but he slid both into his pockets. His shoulders were bent and he turned his head to one side. He was trying hard to pretend he didn't have a sister tugging at his hand, but it was like the fake sneer. It wasn't working.

He looks different, I said again.

Jared is Jared, and he's part of The Problem. One-third, to be exact.

"The Problem" is Sean's word for all the trouble Joined at the Hip caused and would keep causing. But when Sean said **one-third**, I knew what was wrong. Jared wasn't Joined at the Hip when he was alone. Without Ryan and Med, he was Just Jared.

Watson barked. The squirrel had gotten away. The bowl of chips wasn't as lucky.

No, Watson! Drop it! Sean ran toward him.

I watched Sean try to pull what was left of the bowl out of Watson's mouth. Then I scanned the park, but I couldn't see Jared or his sister anywhere. He was gone, but he hadn't vanished. The bunny would be back.

I was walking to the Vault when I saw a pair of old shoes that weren't shoes anymore. Shoes are for walking and you couldn't walk in those things. Near them was a coffee cup that was still a coffee cup. Inside the coffee cup were some coins. Next to the coffee cup was a small cardboard sign on top of a milk crate.

I kept walking.

Spare some change?

I turned around and saw a woman in bare feet and baggy clothes. The *Back in 5 Minutes* sign was gone. She was sitting on the milk crate, drinking coffee from a second cup. She held the cup in both hands and closed her eyes when she took a sip. I stared at her.

I'm savin' my money up.

She reached for the coffee cup with the coins in it and shook it. She smiled.

I'm going to buy a dishwasher. I'm tired of doing dishes.

She took another sip of coffee.

You gonna help me buy a dishwasher?

The homeless woman was looking at me the same way some teachers look at me: like my scars have scarred my brain so I must live in another world. That's what Ms. Garvey once said. *You're in another world, T—. And I need you back in this one.* Then everyone laughed until Ms. Garvey snipped the laughter with a stare.

I shook my head at the homeless woman.

You hungry?

I shook my head again.

You got anything to eat?

All I had was the adopted muffin. I fished it out of my backpack and held it up.

You gonna hold that like some prize or toss it to me?

I tossed it. She caught it, sniffed it, then took a small bite.

Tastes weird.

I didn't disagree.

Didn't say weird was bad. She looked at the unmuffin like she was waiting for it to speak. **You think we should outlaw weird?**

She popped the rest of it into her mouth before I could even shrug. She took another sip of her coffee and raised her cup.

Helps to wash it down with a good cup of joe. She grinned a gray-teeth grin. **Kenyan roast.** She took another sip. **You ever been to Kenya?**

I shook my head.

I have. Twice. She looked at me. **Can you talk?**

I nodded.

You come with batteries?

I shook my head.

Didn't think so. Tell me something. She motioned at me with a finger to get closer. I didn't want to get too close. **You got any lipstick?**

I don't wear lipstick, I said.

Neither do I. It's for my signs.

She pointed to a stack of cardboard signs leaning against a wall. The first one said *Pay-As-You-Go*.

I'm thinking of sprucing 'em up with a few kisses. She made a kissing sound. Then she laughed. **No batteries. No lipstick. What're you good for?**

I knew I was good for a few things but I didn't feel like standing around and making a list. I started to walk away.

Hey! she said.

Then she swore at me. She called me a name I hadn't heard before. I hoped no one I knew was around, because if they were, they might add the name to the names they already call me, and that's a long list.

I stopped and turned around.

A rose by any other name, I said, **would smell as sweet**.

I don't know why I said it. Mr. Binsley force-fed us Shakespeare for a month, and the only thing I remembered was when he talked about roses and said a name doesn't change what you are. Shakespeare was right. A scarred rose is still a rose.

The homeless woman started to laugh.

Romeo, Romeo! Wherefore art thou Romeo?

I took a step forward. **I'm not Romeo!**

I'm not Juliet. She pushed some greasy hair back behind her ear. **In case you were wondering.**

She winked. More laughter.

I headed to the Vault.

Hey! she yelled.

I turned around.

Thank you. For whatever that was I ate. She wiped her mouth. **What the hell was it?**

I shrugged. **I think it was a muffin.**

She smiled. **You got anything else you're not sure about, you know where to find me.**

I nodded and walked away. There were a ton of things I wasn't sure about. I had more questions than spare change.

This is my binder.
These are my photographs.
This is what Ms. Karamath suggested I do.
So I'm doing it.

The Vault isn't really a vault. It's a room inside the Goodison Building. That's the name written in stone over the front doors. I don't know who Mr. Goodison was, but I bet he had a ton of money. They never name buildings after people with no money. It was built in 1906 and was probably once a busy building with lots of busy people doing busy work. Now it's funeral-quiet, without the sniffling.

I rode past the Goodison Building a thousand times on my bike and never gave it a second thought until I started thinking about a special place for my pictures. I wanted a no-one-will-ever-find-it space for photographs I didn't want to keep stuffed in a shoe box beneath my bed. I was always worried my mother would walk into my room and catch me looking at them. But no one looks twice at the Goodison Building because it has missing windows and broken windows and boarded-up windows. I wanted to be alone with my photos, and "alone" and "abandoned" go together.

The front door of the Goodison Building is covered with plywood but it's still a door. When you step in, it smells like an old sweater that was left in the rain for two months. Some homeless people use the main floor. I never see them but I see their homelessness. Old clothes and cardboard beds and rusty shopping carts. No one is going to push a cart up a staircase, so I looked for a place on the second floor. That's where I discovered the room I call the Vault.

The Vault used to be an office. There's still an old calendar on the wall from 1972. Right above *June 1972* is a picture of a woman with a plastic smile, standing beside a shiny car. In one corner there's a bulbless stand-up lamp that can barely stand. I found it on the street. Sean helped me carry up an old truck seat that's as comfortable as a couch. I sit on the driver's side to do my homework. The passenger side is perfect for reading. There was a small tear in between with some foam guts sticking out, but I taped it up.

On a small table is a bread box where I keep things that my mother would tell me to toss if she saw them in my room. A fishing spool. A cracked alarm clock. A rusty locket with a heart-shaped photograph of a man with a rusting smile.

Then there are the photographs. After the accident my parents bought me a bunch of stuff they thought would make me feel better.

But now the aquarium is filled with pictures of fish, the telescope hasn't seen a star in years, and the guitar is missing two strings. Only the camera stuck and never let go.

I've taken hundreds of photos and wallpapered my bedroom and the Vault with them. But I don't just stick pictures to walls. I make themes, just like a gallery with fancy lighting where photographs sell for a ton of money and everyone talks in quiet voices. There are eight photographs in the *Doorknob* section. The first day of the school year Ryan called me a doorknob. Med and Jared laughed and kept saying *Doorknob* as they shook their heads. After that I took a whole bunch of pictures of doorknobs. They're not something anyone ever thinks about but you would miss them as soon as they were gone.

Two rows on a Vault wall are filled with laughter. *Laughter is the best medicine*, Mr. Binsley says. He has about a million expressions that he uses whenever he wants to make a point. I'd take a dose of laughter over a spoonful of gag any day. The laughter I hear when I look at my people-cracking-up photographs is the best kind of laughter. It's this all-you-can-eat sauce that turns sour into sweet and sweet into sweeter.

One wall is covered with Before-and-After photographs I found online. The Before shots are of people with faces that are stare magnets. Funny-looking eyes and funny-looking mouths and missing noses. In the After photographs they look a heck of a lot better. The eyes are closer to where they belong and the mouths look more like mouths. The noses aren't perfect but you could tell the person is way happier with a C+ nose than no nose at all.

The last wall in the Vault is covered with pictures of people with nasty burns. I found most of the pictures on the Internet. There are pictures of old burned people and young burned people and people who are so badly burned you can't tell if they're young or old. What I see on that wall is that I could have had it worse. A lot worse. In one of my favorite photographs a woman is smiling. It's not a normal smile because she doesn't have normal lips but she doesn't seem to care. It was on my wall for a long time before I realized why I liked it. She's saying you can't burn a smile.

That's another reason why I love photographs. They can say things you didn't hear the first time you looked at them.

I once heard my parents tell friends of theirs that *this photography thing is a mixed blessing.* I know there are a lot of days when they feel it's more mixed than blessing.

What I can't figure out, my father says, *is why you can't take more normal pictures. I mean, what is that?*

He pointed to a photograph of a deflated balloon, so flat it looked stuck to the wet road it had landed on. I told him it was a balloon.

I can see that. What I'm trying to understand is why you can't take a picture of a balloon where it belongs. In the air. At the end of a string.

Some days I feel like a photograph my father doesn't get.

My mother says some of my photographs are *painful to look at* but then she always adds, *in a good way,* which is something only a parent would say. Once when we were in the kitchen she said the photograph of an old woman holding a torn and bent umbrella *always gets to me.* I thought I saw almost-tears in her eyes and she smiled and said it was because she was chopping onions. I told her it was celery. *So it is,* she said. She kept chopping and then softly said, *You can't blame her.*

I didn't ask *Blame her for what?* because in our house the word "blame" is a hot potato that's more hot than potato. My mother blames herself for my scars. When I was eight, she thought I was old enough to understand *the whole story* about what had happened to me two years earlier. She started by telling me she had decided to let a pot of applesauce get even saucier, so she kept the front burner on low instead of turning it off.

If only I had turned it off. I —

Then she stopped. She tried talking but the words got stuck in her throat. That was five years ago, and the stuck words haven't moved. I thought she would have run out of blame by now but it's like Ryan's charm. There doesn't seem to be any end to it. Some days she's filled with so much of the stuff it spills out and she blames anyone in blaming distance.

Sometimes that anyone is me. There were times I deserved the blame but a lot of times she dished it out even when I was blameless.

It was unfair but try telling that to the blamer. The more I was blamed, the more I kept things to myself.

That's one reason why I like spending time in the Vault. There's no one around with a head-scratching opinion about my photographs or a plate full of blame because no one else steps inside, not even Sean. He knows I need a place of my own. I sit there on my truckless truck seat, alone but never afraid. The Vault is a safe spot for my burn photographs and a burned me.

I took nine photographs off the Vault walls and chose four to show Ms. Karamath.

You have to take a lot of photographs for one to stick. And not just to a wall.

Before I could get to the library the next morning, I had to get past Mr. Bianco, the principal. He's always at the front doors by 8:00 a.m. and I was there at 8:02.

What brings you here at this hour?

I explained that Ms. Karamath had asked to see some of my photographs.

Bubbles Bianco nodded and started talking about extracurricular activities. I didn't listen because he has this way of using a ton of words but not really saying anything. His words float and burst and disappear. That's why Sean and I call him Bubbles Bianco.

He placed his hand on my shoulder and said, **Did you have anything to do with that window business?**

Two weeks before, late at night, someone broke seven windows in the cafeteria. The next day Bubbles Bianco gathered the whole school at an assembly to talk about *accountability* because *no one had taken responsibility* for the broken windows. Then he bubbled on for another fifteen minutes. At the end he said he expected *a full accounting* by the end of the day.

If he was hoping for the truth to show up at his office, he'd still be there, bobbing in a sea of bubbles. Everyone knew Mitchell Triggs did it. Mitchell always has the same look on his face, like he's this *Y* in a world of vowels and isn't sure he belongs. But Ryan does something that makes him feel he does belong, because he follows Ryan everywhere. So no one said anything about Mitchell breaking the windows, because everyone also knew that if you messed with Ryan, things could get very messy very soon.

Ryan can get away with a lot of things because he's supersmart. He announced in first grade that he wanted to be a doctor, and you can bet one day he'll charm a disease into curing itself. He started getting into my face after my accident and never stopped. As we got older, his schemes became scheme-ier. He stuffed a sweatshirt from the lost-and-found into my backpack and said I had called it want-and-take. He blocked a toilet with pages torn from my science project until it overflowed. He tossed a match onto a bed of straw in a hamster cage and hid the matchbox in my desk. Ryan always made sure he got there in the nick of time and I got nicked.

Every time we ended up in Bubbles Bianco's office, Bubbles took Ryan's smooth words over my stop-and-start explanations. Once, he brought in a school social worker for a meeting with my parents. She said, *Call me Sarah*, and asked me if I was angry about the scars. I didn't tell her it was Ryan that made me angry. She nodded a lot, took a lot of notes, and told my parents I needed to find *positive, constructive ways to channel my feelings.* That's when they bought me the aquarium and the telescope and the guitar. When I said I hadn't done anything wrong, I had a feeling they only half believed me, because my mother said she wouldn't blame me if I had. My father said I should drop the finger-pointing and take the high road, which he was sure Ryan would share. The way my parents saw it, I was a problem to be solved and Ryan was the perfect solution.

I didn't have anything to do with the broken windows, I told Bubbles Bianco.

He grunted, but it was hard to tell what the grunt meant. I could see he had some doubts but they weren't too big to step over. So he nodded and let me go. I headed to the library.

I showed Ms. Karamath four photographs.

First photograph. *Bicycle in Snowdrift.*

One night there was a freak storm and in the morning I took a photograph of this bicycle. It's like the ghost of a bike, here but not here. It reminds me of shipwrecks found at the bottom of the ocean, only instead of sand, the bike is half-buried in snow. It makes me think of a story that ends before it's over. There's no *And then.*

Second photograph.

Birds of a feather flock together is one of the million expressions Mr. Binsley uses to make a point. Some of the birds look like they're flying in pairs. Some look like they want to be on their own. Some are so close together they look like one bird. Some look like planes. A few look like minnows. They all look like they belong. I call it *Joined at the Wing.*

Third photograph.

I took it in front of the Pet Palace. The girl's mother kept telling her to *Smile! Smile!* but the smile looked rehearsed. A minute after I took the picture, the woman poked the plastic bag with her finger.

How long will this one last before it's flushed down the toilet?

The girl burst into tears.

There's something there, Ms. Karamath said after I laid *Girl with Goldfish* down on a library table.

Where? I asked.

She just kept staring at the photographs. **You've captured a moment**, she finally said. As if a moment had four legs and sharp fangs and I had trapped one.

I showed Ms. Karamath the last photograph.

When I asked Woman with Painted Eyebrows if I could take a picture she said, *Of course. But Mr. Jackson has to be in it too.* You can't tell by looking at the photograph that she never lets go of Mr. Jackson. She never takes him for a walk. She takes him for a hold.

Ms. Karamath looked at the picture like she was reading a recipe with an ingredient she had never heard of, something Sean's mother would use to bake muffins.

These are very good, T—.

What I heard was *You've got flow.* I'm still waiting for a growth spurt, but just then I gained about an inch of proud.

Do you know Diane Arbus?

I racked my brain. **The redheaded girl with really long braids in Miss Calnan's class?**

Ms. Karamath smiled and shook her head. **She's a photographer. You might like her work.**

She described some of Diane Arbus's photographs. The titles sounded interesting. *Masked Woman in a Wheelchair. A Jewish Giant at Home with His Parents in the Bronx. Mexican Dwarf in His Hotel Room.* I wrote all the names down in my head.

Why do you think I would like her photographs?

Ms. Karamath looked away, then looked at me. **It's how you see the world.**

The more she described Diane Arbus the more I wanted to meet her. Until she told me she was dead.

There are no books of Diane Arbus's pictures in the school library. When I asked Ms. Karamath why, she said it was out of her hands. When I asked what that meant she said, **It's all about red tape** and that it wasn't something I had to worry about. "Red tape" is just another way of saying there are too many rules. Every rule is another layer on top of the truth, and soon there are so many layers there's no point digging anymore. Your fingers will bleed. You will never get the whole picture.

You might find her work at the public library, Ms. Karamath said. Then she explained that Diane Arbus had committed suicide **but her photographs are very much alive**.

That's another kind of flow Mr. Ramshaw would never understand. A photograph keeps going long after the photographer is gone.

Next to the milk crate was a cardboard sign — *Ask About Our Mortgage Rates* — but no one was there to ask.

Two blocks later I heard a familiar voice.

Hey, Romeo!

I turned around but didn't see her.

Over here.

I looked both ways. I heard a clanking sound.

Follow the yellow brick road.

I followed the clank until I reached a laneway. Not Juliet was bent over a bin, plucking aluminum cans and tossing them into a large, clear plastic bag.

Good to see you, Romeo.

My name isn't Romeo.

Wanna know mine?

She smiled a big smile. Her teeth looked museum-old. She didn't care. She kept smiling, like admission was free.

Lucy.

I didn't think she was making it up. Some people have a hard time putting lies into their mouths. They don't fit, no matter what the size.

You gonna stand there or you gonna help me sort?

I'm going to the library.

Lucy half-crushed a can with both hands.

Library's not going anywhere. But I am. Her bag rattled when she gave it a small kick. **You gonna stand or sort?**

I sorted.

She didn't say a word for about twenty cans. Then she held up a dented can.

Know what this is? She didn't wait for me to answer. **Freedom.**

I had no idea what freedom tasted like but I didn't think it was cherry flavored.

What kind of freedom? I asked.

Lucy didn't reply. She was sucking on a can of root beer. She squeezed out every last drop, then tossed the can into the plastic bag and wiped her mouth with the back of her hand.

The freedom to not have to wait all day for a cup full of spare change. See, some days I make enough for a ticket to the opera.

She smiled. I smiled back.

But others there's barely enough for a spoonful of caviar. Those days I go hunting. Sorting cans is messy but it's quick cash. She picked up a can. **Easy money.**

She didn't say much more after that. A half hour and two bins later, Lucy's bag was full. She flung it over her shoulder and grinned.

I feel like Santa Claus, she said. **Follow me.**

I didn't know where she was going but I walked behind her. She got a ton of stares and snickers but she shook them all off. A few stuck to me.

Lucy suddenly stopped. I had kept my head down to dodge the stares. When I looked up I saw Owen, a Ryan-in-training, hyena-laughing as he took pictures of Lucy with his cell phone. Owen will do whatever it takes to get to Ryan's hip.

Wait till they see this!

I knew who "they" were. I pictured the usual crew huddled around Owen's cell phone as Ryan stirred the snickers.

34

Lucy laid her bag of cans down onto the sidewalk and posed for him. **I'm ready for my close-up.**

Owen smiled a Mount Rushmore smile — *I'm big, you're small* — and took more pictures. When Lucy stopped posing, Owen kept shooting. He only stopped when I took a picture of him taking pictures of Lucy. He gave me a dirty look but I'd seen dirtier. Owen walked away, laughing again as he thumbed through the pictures on his phone.

Lucy looked like I felt after a Ryan arm-twist. No bruises, but it still stung. I asked her if I could take a different kind of photograph than the ones Owen had taken.

She shrugged. **A photograph is a photograph.**

I disagreed but I kept my thoughts to myself.

Lucy stared at something for about a week before she said, **Time to cash in.**

No one really noticed us when we stepped into the supermarket. Lucy walked up to something that looked like a vending machine, only this thing swallowed empty cans. She fed it can after can. By the time the bag was empty, she was $14.55 richer.

Outside the supermarket, she held out four dollars.

Take it.

I shook my head.

It's yours.

I'm not homeless, I unsaid. *I don't sit on a milk crate all day.*

I owe you.

I didn't know what she was talking about. I tried looking at Lucy without looking at her. Her face was a head-scratching mystery. A few deep lines. A small scar. Something that might have been dried blood. It was hard to tell how old she was.

Lucy wedged the four dollars into my closed hand.

Before. What you did. You stopped him.

She pointed to my camera.

That thing comes in handy, doesn't it?

I guess. I didn't know what else to say.

Safer than a knife, right? Put him in his place. You pull out a camera, makes people think twice.

I nodded, though I wasn't sure a camera was much of a weapon. It had stopped Owen that time, but he only really stops when Ryan tells him to. I slid the four dollars into my pocket, thanked Lucy, and walked away.

Wanna take another picture?

I shook my head and kept walking.

Want me to take yours?

I stopped.

Lemme take your picture.

I've taken thousands of pictures of other people. This was the first time someone had asked to take a picture of me.

Why? I asked.

Lucy started to laugh. This wasn't bow-and-arrow laughter where I'm the target. This wasn't nail-and-hammer laughter where I'm the plank. This wasn't the sour laughter I'd heard before. This laughter was thick gravy you pour over platefuls of grief to disguise the taste.

She looked at me with her gray-teeth grin and said, **Why not?**

Because of the way I look, I unsaid. I shrugged.

Gimme your camera and tell me what to do.

I showed Lucy how my camera works. She was like a kid with a new toy.

When I was growing up Polaroid was the big thing. A picture, appearing right before your eyes. I couldn't believe it.

I couldn't imagine Lucy as Little Lucy, with a normal face and a normal smell.

She took about a thousand practice pictures so she could **get the hang of it**. Some people looked at her and laughed. It wasn't gravy laughter but Lucy didn't seem to care. Then she took ten pictures of me. I told her that's all I wanted. We looked at the pictures together.

These are all black-and-white.

I nodded.

This thing can't take color?

I told her it could.

Then why don't you?

Color is more colorful, I said. **Black-and-white is more revealing.**

I read that in this book my grandmother gave me called *Cameras and Conversations*. Lucy nodded.

I looked like a doofus in every single shot but Lucy didn't seem to notice. All she said over and over again was **Nice.** I didn't know if she thought I looked nice or if she thought she had done nice work. I didn't ask.

She handed me my camera, turned around, and walked away. I followed her for a few steps, then stopped. I wondered where she lived. I wondered if she slept under a cardboard roof or curled like a cat in the corner of a shelter. I didn't know where she went and what she did when she wasn't sitting on her milk crate, asking for spare change. I had a feeling she was a many-sided Lucy with sides she didn't want anyone to see.

I didn't expect to see her wave-good-bye side.

Before I knew it, I was waving back.

First I heard it. Then I saw it. A rescue pumper, with a get-out-of-my-way siren. It was like the fire truck was Moses and everything in its way was the Red Sea.

As I ran toward the fire, I wondered where it registered on the Zito scale. Earthquakes have the Richter scale to measure how big the earthquake is, and hurricanes get names like Katrina and Sandy, but the truth is, you can count a five-alarm fire on one hand. Fires deserve as much as earthquakes, so I made up the Zito scale. It starts at 100 points for shed-in-laneway fires and climbs to 1000 for the-building-is-toast blazes. Joseph Zito was an elevator operator in a building in New York about a thousand years ago. The building caught on fire, and a lot of women sewing shirts on the upper floors were trapped inside because the doors were locked so no one could leave early.

That's something Ryan would have done. There have always been Ryans around, dishing out grief long before there were dishes. Caveman Ryan. Gladiator Ryan. Knight-in-shining-armor Ryan. Homesteader Ryan. Lock-the-factory-doors Ryan.

Joseph Zito was the opposite of Ryan. He went up and down, in and out of the flames, and saved more than a hundred and fifty people. There have always been Zitos around too, but the Ryans get a heck of a lot more attention.

By the time I reached the fire, some firefighters were already walking out the front doors of the apartment building, back toward their trucks. It must have been a false alarm. A woman next to me scanned each of the three floors. She was wearing sparkly glasses with half the sparkles missing.

Nothing, she said. I could tell she was disappointed. **Not a lick of flames. No smoke neither.** She sucked on her teeth. **A waste of time.**

I knew what she meant. She was a moth like me — a person drawn to fires. I didn't say anything though. I could tell she was the type who would talk my ear off, smack her lips, and then start on the other ear. Sparkles turned around and walked away. She patted a firefighter on the shoulder as she went, a *Sorry for your trouble* pat. He gave her a *What the heck?* look but she didn't notice. She kept on walking.

I looked back at the apartment building. I didn't want anyone to get hurt or freak out about a lost pet or end up on television, bawling their eyes out. But I was hoping for some flames. I like watching fires. Fires don't care if you're rich or poor, if you're right or wrong, if you're a supermodel or super ugly. Fire is blind.

I figured you'd never want to go near a fire, Sean once said. *After what happened.*

I knew what he meant. You would think because of my accident I would run away from fires, not toward them. But if you ask me, the only way you can understand anything is to get close to it. I try to get as close to flames as I can. Maybe one day they'll tell me something.

The firefighters started to load their gear back onto the trucks. They didn't look disappointed. They didn't look relieved. They looked like it was all in a day's work, which can be a real workout when you're fighting fires that don't follow any rules.

You should thank me.

I turned around. Ryan was alone. I tried to pretend I wasn't surprised to see him, but I could tell by the look on his face that mine had surprise written all over it.

Weren't expecting me, were you?

Ryan didn't wait for me to answer.

I knew you'd be here. 'Cause everyone knows you got fire on the brain. Not to mention other places.

He rubbed his neck in the spot where my neck has the leathery scars. He smiled. Then he touched his cheek.

I was around way before these guys showed up. He pointed to a fire truck as it rolled away. **Wonder how?**

I started to say something but Ryan kept going. When he's driving a conversation, he doesn't stop until he's finished. He doesn't care what he runs over.

I pulled the alarm. He flicked a switch in the air. **I knew the trucks would be here in no time. And you'd be right behind, wagging your tail.**

He put his elbow on top of my shoulder. I stepped away. He grinned.

So where's my thank-you?

You can take a head-to-toe X-ray. Donate my organs. Turn me inside out. You'll never find a thank you in me for Ryan.

I know what you're thinking.

I still hadn't said a word.

You're thinking, "Boo hoo hoo. False alarm. I want a fire. I want the real deal."

Ryan leaned in close. I could feel his breath against the normal side of my neck.

Maybe next time, he whispered. **Maybe something closer to home.**

It was only a whisper but I felt a ringing in my ears. He turned around and walked away, then turned back.

One more thing.

He grinned.

I saved your ass.

He waved to a police officer who was talking to a firefighter.

That there is Sergeant Chomack. He wants you to stay put until he has a word with you. Ryan's grin grew as the Sergeant Chomack walked toward us. **I told him you pulled the alarm.**

I felt my stomach twist into knots. Ryan shoulder-punched me like we were old friends. Sergeant Chomack approached. His eyes and mouth were tight and all business.

Listen up and listen hard, Sergeant Chomack said. **Your friend told me you're behind all this trouble. That this wasn't the first time you pulled this kind of stunt. I'm telling you, it's the last.** He moved in nose-to-nose in order to make his point. **We clear?**

I nodded.

False alarms cost time. They cost money. He turned to Ryan. **Tell your friend here what the greatest cost is.**

Ryan wore this very serious look. **They can be fatal.**

Fatal is fatal, Sergeant Chomack said. **There are no second chances. Understood?**

I looked at Ryan. He had just swallowed a smirk.

Understood, I said.

I'm going to give you a second chance 'cause your pal swore six ways to Sunday that he'll keep an eye on you. That it will never happen again. Sergeant Chomack planted a firm hand on my shoulder. **You got something to say to him?**

I looked at Ryan and wanted to scream. There was no way my word would be taken over his. It's hard to beat a winning smile with no scars.

Thanks, I said to Ryan, as softly as I could.

He shrugged it off. **It was nothing.** He asked Sergeant Chomack if he could leave because he volunteered **at a clinic for kids with cancer.**

Absolutely.

Ryan ran off. Sergeant Chomack turned toward me.

Listen up. Your name's in the system and on my radar. Don't let this happen again. He stared at me, then walked away.

The fire was a false alarm but I was burning inside.

By the time I got to the library, the fire that had burned inside me wasn't much more than a pile of embers.

Sean and I didn't really belong at the Wilcott Street Library. Most of the people there were old men with yellow teeth and big, hound-dog ears who fell asleep reading newspapers. But neither of us was bothered by their soft snores. Sean got wrapped up in a mystery novel about a forensic accountant.

I was knocked over and knocked out by Diane Arbus.

I had never seen photographs like hers before. They were pictures of people who all looked weird or had something funny about them. One of the photographs is called *Child with Toy Hand Grenade in Central Park, NYC, 1962*. It's a picture of a boy standing in a park. He's wearing these shorts that have straps on them and one of the straps has fallen off his shoulders, but the boy doesn't look like he notices or cares. The fingers in his left hand are all tense, like a mechanical claw. In his right hand is the toy grenade that the title says he's holding. The boy has a look on his face like he's about to explode.

Some days I know exactly how he feels. Only I grab my camera instead of a grenade.

Ms. Karamath had described *Mexican Dwarf in His Hotel Room, NYC, 1970*. Now I saw it for myself. The dwarf is sitting on a bed. He's got a big, wide smile that looks even bigger and wider because of this thin mustache that seems like it's been drawn on with a marker. He's wearing a hat, the kind of hat that men wore a million years ago when men wore hats to work. He's leaning against a night table and you can see a bottle of liquor to one side. His head is too big for his body, but his body doesn't seem to mind. One foot sticks out from beneath a towel that covers him from the waist down. He must have eaten grief at least once a day, because you can't be a dwarf and not eat grief. But he must have finished his helping of grief long before Diane Arbus took his picture because he looks happy. Way happier than the kid in Central Park.

I stared at the photograph of the happy dwarf for about seven weeks, trying to figure out how I felt. My feelings were pinballing all over the place. I was confused. I was jealous. I was hooked.

If you ask me, a grief-eating dwarf shouldn't look that happy. Maybe that's the "something" in the *something there*, which is what Ms. Karamath said when she looked at my photographs — the something you see but can't explain. I'm still figuring it out myself, but I think it's about creating opposites within one picture. A lot of dwarfs must overdose on stares, but this one looks like he eats stares for breakfast. Same thing with the kid in Central Park. Grenades are deadly but it's the kid who looks like a lit fuse.

I flipped back to the front page of the book and something Diane Arbus said there. *A photograph is a secret about a secret. The more it tells you the less you know.* You would think the more you're told the more you would know, but Diane Arbus said the opposite, and that's one reason why I like her photographs. Opposites make you look in different directions, and I like spending time in the spot where they go their separate ways.

This guy two tables over stood up and started yelling, **Drop your bag!**

Drop your bag! Drop your bag!

He had one of those faces that seemed young and old at the same time, with soft, baby-cow eyes and creases in his cheeks. His long hair looked pasted to a baseball cap and his jacket was buttoned right to the top. He belonged in a Diane Arbus photo. Sean looked at me as if I knew him and should make an introduction.

What's in the bag?!

The man was having a conversation with himself, which is a heck of a lot better than a lot of conversations because at least he knew he was being listened to. Half the people in the library looked too old to hear him or to care.

Open the bag!

There was no bag. A librarian approached him but stopped when he stabbed at the air with a bent finger. Sean looked at me again. I shrugged. Sean stood up and pulled a water bottle out of his backpack.

Sir, would you like something to drink?

Bag Man stared at Sean with glassy eyes. From the look on his face, he had been called a lot of things in his life but "sir" wasn't one of them.

Put the bag down! he yelled.

Sean took a few steps forward and then stopped at the end of Bag Man's table. He held out the water. **Sir?**

Bag Man looked at the bottle like it had wings and was going to take off. Sean uncapped the bottle, placed it on the table, and stepped away. Bag Man grabbed it and guzzled down the water.

Someone clapped, as if the show was over. The librarian thanked Sean and then took a seat beside Bag Man and asked him his name.

I heard him say **Sidney**. By the time I checked out the Diane Arbus book, Sidney was talking to the librarian like they were old friends.

Where did you learn to do that? I asked Sean as soon as we stepped out of the library. **It's like he was on fire and you put it out. You know. With the water.**

Sean shrugged. **It was in a movie I saw. But it wasn't a bottle of water. It was an orange.**

Sean described this scene where a woman is going to throw herself off a bridge. This young cop and this old cop get there and the old cop starts talking but she's not listening. The not-listening goes on for about ten minutes. The woman is about to toss herself into the deep water below when the old cop pulls an orange out of his pocket and offers it to her. They start talking about the orange and soon they're talking about other things, and after about twenty minutes of orange and non-orange talk, the woman climbs down and the orange is peeled.

Then the young cop slaps the old cop on the back for saving the woman's life. All the old cop says is "It's not about the orange."

I pictured the woman sitting next to the old cop, wrapped in a blanket, eating the orange and giving him a slice. **Then what's it about?**

Sean said he wasn't sure. **But I didn't have an orange in my backpack so I thought I'd try my water bottle.**

I thought about the grenade-holding kid in Central Park. He could have used a Sean.

Hey!

Lucy called out to me as I headed home from the library. She was in a laneway, waving with a book in one hand.

Almost done with the chapter, she said as I walked up to her. Her book was called *Anna Karenina*.

What's that you got?

I was holding the Diane Arbus book. I showed her the cover. **It's a book.**

Lucy smiled her stained smile. **I didn't think it was a toaster. What kind?**

A book of photographs.

What kind?

Most conversations aren't really conversations because a lot of people like to be heard but don't want to listen. They do all the driving, steering the conversations down one-way streets. When you point to a two-way street, they stop driving. Lucy looked like she would drive in any direction.

They're by Diane Arbus.

Lucy put *Anna* away and patted the concrete next to her as if it was a comfy couch. **Have a seat.**

I sat down beside her and gave her the book.

She spent a day looking at the first photograph before she flipped the page and took in the second. I had to check to make sure there were no words in the book because it seemed like she was reading each page. She stared at each picture for a very long time. Sometimes she would grunt a caveman grunt, just like my father whenever he looked at the pictures on my wall. Then she would turn the page and start all over again. She moved her fingers across some of the pictures the way a blind person reads Braille.

She stopped at one picture of two women with faces a lot of people can't face. Those people would rather laugh a quick laugh than take a long look. Both of the women wear these hats with flowers on top that are tied beneath their chins with bows. One of the women has a big smile and is missing her front teeth. She clasps her hands together like she doesn't have a care in the world, a purse hanging from her arm. The woman beside her is holding on to her other arm and wears a sweater with the top buttons all done up. But the rest of the buttons are undone so her sweater looks like a tent.

Lucy stared at that picture for about a week. She nodded and said, **They found each other.**

I didn't know what to say but I knew I wanted to say something. **Found?**

Lucy looked up. **They understand each other.**

That sounded right.

You frame 'em yet? Lucy pointed to my camera. **The pictures I took of you.**

I deleted them, I unsaid.

You're a good photographer, I said.

Lucy laughed. I wished I could carry her laugh with me the way some people carry water bottles. I could sprinkle it on half stares.

The hell I am. She handed me the Diane Arbus book. *She's a good photographer. I bet you are too.*

I shrugged. **I'm still learning.**

Lucy stood up and put her hands on her hips. She smiled this gravel smile like she was posing for the cover of a magazine you see in supermarkets, full of famous people with perfect teeth. She motioned for me to stand so we were face-to-face. Her face was way more interesting than a book but harder to read.

Show me some love. She tapped my camera. **Take me back to Vegas.**

She told me she had once been a showgirl in Las Vegas. She blew kisses at the camera, kicked her feet in the air, and danced down the laneway until she reached the sidewalk. A lot of people stopped and gave her *What the heck?* looks but Lucy didn't care. She kicked the stares away and kicked her way back down toward me.

It wasn't Vegas, unless Vegas smells like burned rubber and beer bottles. But Lucy danced like she was on the middle of a bright-light stage, lost in music no one else could hear. It wasn't the dark-forest kind of lost where you wish you were home and warm. Lucy looked like she was happy to be lost, like she didn't want to go back to wherever she started from.

I took a ton of pictures of Lucy dancing in the laneway.

Halfway through the second ton, Lucy grabbed my hand.

Let's dance.

I told her I didn't know how to dance.

You don't need to be a fish to swim. She grinned her gray-teeth grin. **My mother drilled that into me when I was a kid.**

I tried to picture Little Lucy again but didn't get very far before she took my camera and placed it on a ledge as if it was an egg. After five minutes of the foxtrot (more tripping than trotting), Lucy held both of my hands and spun me around until everything was a dizzy blur. She started to laugh and then I started to laugh. The faster we spun the more we laughed. We lost our balance and fell to the ground. We kept laughing until we ran out of laughter.

Tell me what you think of this.

Ms. Karamath showed me a picture of a totally naked girl, screaming. It looks like she's running for her life down a road. She asked me if I ever heard of the Vietnam War and I nodded but I didn't know a heck of a lot about it. After a while all these wars start blending together. There's this battle and that battle and a bunch of dates. In the end, they're about dead people and days on a calendar when people say we should remember the dead people so it doesn't happen again, but the truth is it does happen again.

She told me it was a famous photograph from the war, and that **photographs can Make a Difference**. Ms. Karamath is big on Making a Difference. She puts up pictures and stories on the library walls about kids who are Making a Difference. There's a girl who started collecting old sleeping bags and giving them to homeless people. A boy who invented a special can opener for people who are too weak to open cans by themselves. A class that raised money so that kids in some poor country could buy pencils and notebooks. Every month Ms. Karamath puts up a new batch of Making a Difference stories. Some kids say things like *I'd rather make a sundae* and that always gets a big laugh, unless Ms. Karamath is around. Then the laughter gets buried so quickly there's no time for a funeral.

I asked Ms. Karamath if the girl in the picture was dead. She said she was alive and an adult now because the Vietnam War was a long time ago. I asked her why the girl was running and screaming. She said her village had been attacked by Napalm and that this picture was seen around the world.

It put a face on the war in Vietnam.

Who was Napalm?

I figured Napalm was like Hitler. First-name famous people are usually popular, like Elvis and Jesus, and last-name-only famous people like Hitler and Frankenstein are usually nasty pieces of work.

Ms. Karamath explained that napalm wasn't a person but a chemical that was used during the Vietnam War.

I asked her if the picture had a title and she said she didn't think so. **What would you name this photograph?**

I thought of a bunch of names. *Naked Girl Running. Napalm Is No Fun. Girl Screaming.*

Names are important, **T—** Ms. Karamath said.

As if I didn't know that. After I started getting stung with names, I twisted their sharp ends into something too round to cut. In the first grade I turned *Moron!* into Morondo. In fifth grade, *Retard!* became Retardo. Adding an *o* softens things. Otherwise we'd say "Hell" every time we answer the phone.

I looked at the photograph. You didn't have to speak Vietnamese to understand it. A scream doesn't have a language.

The Scream, I told Ms. Karamath. **That's what I would call it.**

She smiled. **That's already the name of a famous painting. Let me show you.**

I followed Ms. Karamath to her computer. In about two seconds there was this painting on her screen. The painting is of a person who doesn't really look like a person. He's more like a ghost. The person is covering his ears and screaming as he stands on a bridge by a lake. In the background is a red, wavy sky you would swear was on fire. Some people are walking behind him. It looks like he's running away from them and wants to tear his head off.

It's by Edvard Munch, she said. **Paintings can make a difference too, T—. This one has left its mark for generations.**

I thanked her for showing it to me and took the photograph back to my table. I had barely begun looking at it again when it was snatched out of my hands.

Sweet, Owen said. **The mutant has a picture of his girlfriend naked.**

He showed it to Mitchell and Lee. They smirked. I snatched it back and turned it facedown.

Relax, dipstick. Owen always tried to imitate Ryan. I wondered how far he would go to be joined to Ryan's hip. **Gonna keep it in your locker?**

Mitchell smiled. **Under his pillow.**

Lee nodded. **So he can dream of running away with her.**

All three of them cracked up. Owen tried grabbing a corner of the photograph so he could flip it over and have another look. I covered it with both hands.

What's your girlfriend running from? Her mutant boyfriend?

Ms. Karamath was back at the table before I answered. She looked at Owen with drill-bit eyes.

Are you here to borrow a book?

Just browsing, Lee said.

Then browse, Ms. Karamath said, pointing toward the shelves and shelves of library books. Her voice was flat and cold.

Owen walked away as if browsing was his idea. Mitchell and Lee followed. When they were gone I turned over the photograph of the girl. Ms. Karamath and I both stared at it for a long time.

How far did she run, I unasked, *before she was heard?*

That afternoon I found Lucy about three blocks away from her crate. I wanted to show her the picture of the napalmed girl. I wanted to hear what she had to say about the scream. But she was facing the side of a building, arguing with the brick wall. It was a one-word, one-sided argument. I had a feeling it was a side of Lucy she didn't want me to see.

No!

She yelled **No!** over and over again. Usually they landed one at a time. Sometimes they landed in clusters.

Nononononononoonono!

I gripped the copy of the photograph in my hand.

Lucy started to bang her head against the wall.

No! I yelled.

The size of my **No!** put her **No!** in its place. She stopped to face me. Her forehead was bleeding. She looked at me like I had caught her naked. I don't know who was more uncomfortable.

Go!

I didn't move.

She said **Go!** a thousand more times.

I said **No**, but it wasn't long before her **Go!** was running circles around my **No**. Soon there was no **No!** left, and just Lucy's non-stop **Go!**

I didn't want to leave her like that. I wanted to at least give her something to wipe the blood off her forehead. All I had was the cloth for cleaning my camera lens.

So that's what I gave her.

I didn't think she had any **Go!** left in her.

She did.

I turned around and almost-ran.

Sean invites me over for dinner at his house a couple of times a month. I do the same for him, but if you ask me, dinner at Sean's apartment is way more interesting. At my house, if we're having spaghetti, then what you get is spaghetti. At Sean's house almost every meal comes with a surprise. You never know what ingredients Sean's mother has up her sleeve, and Surprise beats Same every time they face off, even if it takes a half hour to figure out what it is we're eating, and another half hour to chew it.

We were hanging out in Sean's room before dinner. I told him about seeing Lucy bang her head against the brick wall.

Why would she do that? I said.

Sean looked down, as if the answer was somewhere on his bedroom floor. **I don't have a clue. You'd have to ask her.**

I wanted to ask Lucy about a lot of things, but a question about banging her head until it bled wasn't on the list.

She must have been in a lot of pain, Sean said. **In here.** He tapped his head to say broken-mind pain, which is way different than broken-bone pain.

I nodded. **It's like she was punishing herself.** I couldn't imagine what Lucy had done to feel she had deserved that kind of punishment.

What will you do if she does it again?

I don't know. I wasn't sure when it was right to step forward or better to step back. I figured that was a dance you learn when you're older.

Watson yawned. He had been sleeping on Sean's pillow. Sean's a single child and his mother is a single mother and Watson is his single dog. Sean's mother bought him a dog after his father left them when Sean was four. Sean's father is living somewhere else with somebody else, which means Sean sees a heck of a lot more of Watson (night and day) than he sees his father (once in a blue moon, and he stopped checking to see if the moon was blue a long time ago).

One of Sean's walls is filled with photographs I've taken. Some are of Sean. Some are of Watson. Two are of his mother. Most are of Sean and Watson. One of Sean's favorite pictures is *Boy with Dog*. I kept a copy in the Vault.

Watson had found a stuffed lobster in the playground, only this lobster had had the stuffing knocked out of it. Sean thought it would be a good idea to put it into the lost-and-found bin by the clubhouse. Watson disagreed.

Supper's ready!

Watson leaped off Sean's bed and ran in circles in front of the bedroom door. He knew supper meant leftovers for him, only in Sean's apartment it's dropunders. Watson lies beneath the table during every meal and Sean drops him bite-size samples of whatever's being served. Sean's mother doesn't know about dropunders and would be hurt if she did. So Sean waits for the right moment, and Watson is always there, waiting for him.

Sean opened the bedroom door. Watson bolted out. By the time we sat down at the table, Watson was already beneath it. There was a basket of warm buns next to a pot of steaming soup. Sean's mother didn't have a ladle, so she used a measuring cup to pour the soup into our bowls.

What is this? Sean asked. He had scooped up a chunk of something with his spoon. **You said we were having chicken noodle soup.**

We are. That's "chicken" with quotes.

For a second I thought quotes was a kind of noodle until Sean's mother made air quotes with her fingers. I put a spoonful in my mouth. Slowly.

Sean stared at his spoon. **What does that mean?**

His mother smiled. **It's plant-based**, she said proudly.

A rubber plant, I unsaid. It took me about six years to chew one piece.

Sean didn't even pretend to chew. He was halfway through his bowl when he dropped two pieces of chicken-with-quotes beneath the table. I heard Watson pounce.

Sean was buttering a bun and I had begun my third hour of chewing a second piece when Watson started making these funny sounds.

Watson?

Sean peeked under the table but by then Watson was standing by the television, twitching and choking. I didn't think a dog could have a seizure until I saw it with my own eyes.

Oh, my God! Sean's mother said. **Should I call 911?**

I didn't know why she was asking us because usually parents are the ones in charge. But Sean's mother looked as frightened as I felt.

What should we do? I asked Sean.

Sean didn't hear me. He was talking to Watson, stroking his back, talking in a soft voice that was hot-chocolate soothing.

It's okay, buddy. You're going to be okay.

Watson looked like he was a week's drive from okay. He was gasping for air, wheezing like a bent old man and not a trouble-seeking dog.

Try the Heimlich maneuver! Sean's mom said.

I don't think that will work, I said. I prayed she wouldn't suggest mouth-to-mouth resuscitation.

Suddenly Watson made this loud, hacking noise. I thought he was a goner. Then something flew out of his mouth and across the room. Watson slowly became Watson again.

What was that? Sean's mother asked.

Sean picked the thing up off the carpet before she could get a closer look. **Who knows**, he said.

We all looked at Watson, who was wagging his tail.

I never want to go through that again, Sean's mother said, as if she was the one who was one choke away from choking to death. She gave Watson a hug and kissed him on the nose. **You boys up for dessert?**

Watson's ears stood at attention. Sean says Watson may not be the sharpest knife in the drawer, but that drawer is definitely in the kitchen.

Sean thanked his mother but told her he wasn't in the mood. Neither was I. For all I knew, it was "ice cream."

Lucy was Lucy again, sitting next to a stack of her handwritten signs.

I hadn't brought any photographs I had taken of her because I wasn't sure if she would be in the mood to see them. I didn't bring the photograph of Napalm Girl either. I had decided to call it *Napalm Avenue*. I could have called it *Napalm Road*, but "avenue" sounds like a street with big, leafy trees, the kind of place where you might want to live, until you find out what napalm is and see a naked girl running by your window screaming her head off. Only people like Joined at the Hip would have a house on Napalm Avenue. When I told Ms. Karamath what I had called it, she said the title added *a nice touch of irony*. I said, *Thank you*, and pretended I understood what "irony" meant.

Hey, I said to Lucy.

She looked up. **Hey.**

We didn't say anything else for about five weeks. Neither of us mentioned a brick wall but it felt like there was one between us. Finally I asked her if I could take more pictures of her.

Whatever floats your boat, she said. She raised her cup like she was making a toast.

I spent ten boat-floating minutes taking photographs of Lucy. Her sour expression didn't change all that much, so I thought I'd get her something sweet.

Do you like strawberries?

Lucy didn't hesitate. **Love 'em. You gotta patch I should know about?**

Wait here.

Lucy smiled. **I don't have any travel plans, Romeo.**

I had just enough money to buy a small box of strawberries. When I gave them to Lucy she didn't eat them right away. She held them in her hands as if they were rare and beautiful. When she finally took a bite she looked like a kid who was ice-cream-cone-happy. Soon she was all smiles, no strawberries.

Lucy stood up, wiped her mouth with the sleeve, and said, **I'm going to the park. You coming?**

I shrugged. **I guess.**

She grabbed my hand. **We better get moving. It's busy this time of day.**

It wasn't busy. It was a parkette, which is another way of saying "small park." It's meant for small kids but *Small Park for Small Kids* doesn't look great on a sign so this one just said *Linden Parkette*.

Lucy wasn't a kid or small but no one seemed to mind. Even if they did, I had a feeling Lucy was so used to strange looks that they would have to come with sparklers and glow sticks before she noticed them. One girl pointed but her mother tucked her daughter's finger into her hand and that was the end of the point.

Lucy loved going down the slide. The more she did it, the farther she seemed to get away from the Lucy I had seen banging her head against the wall. Up, down, up, down. Twenty minutes later I wondered how much up she had left in her. Ten minutes after that I took a photograph of her sitting at the bottom of the slide. She looked tired. She looked satisfied. She looked like she didn't want to be anywhere else.

Do you come here a lot?

Lucy nodded. **Nighttime, too. I sit over there, give the moon an earful, and don't leave until I'm good and ready.**

She pointed to a small platform you could reach by walking up a few steps or climbing a rope or stepping on metal rungs. She walked to the steps, sat down, and closed her eyes. When she opened them again, she had this faraway look.

By the time she turned to me, the faraway had faded.

We're done here, she said.

Before I knew it, I was following her back to her crate and signs. After she found a spot on the sidewalk she dug her hands into a coat pocket and poured a handful of coins into a coffee cup.

Cash flow, Lucy said. I was happy to see her gray-tooth grin again.

Look what the cat dragged in!

We both looked down the street and saw the same thing: Joined at the Hip. Owen and Lee were trailing right behind Jared and Med. I could tell Ryan was ready to feast and I was the main course. I felt test-day queasy.

Who's your friend? Ryan looked at Lucy as if she had antlers on her head.

I'm Lucy. She looked at Ryan. **Who're you?**

I'm raising money for cancer research, Ryan said as if he meant it. Owen and Med cracked up. **Do you have any spare change?**

Jared and Lee snickered. They didn't sound like real snickers. They sounded like snickers they wanted Ryan to hear.

Ryan grinned. **Look what we have here**, he said. He bent down and picked up Lucy's coffee cup. He opened his hand to catch the coins but when he tipped the cup over, all the loose change scattered onto the sidewalk.

Whoops!

Ryan held out the coffee cup like he was waiting for Lucy to take it. Like he was a guest in Lucy's kitchen and Lucy-the-host had said *Would you care for more?* He was still smiling.

Pick that up, Lucy said. She pointed to the coins scattered on the sidewalk.

I watched Ryan's crew watch Ryan to see what he would do next. People carrying shopping bags and holding briefcases and pushing strollers slowed down as they walked by, but none of them stopped.

Pick that up, Lucy said again.

Ryan tossed the cup to the ground. **Kiss my ass.**

Joined at the Hip laughed. It was bait-and-hook laughter and Lucy was the worm.

Kiss your ass?

Ryan nodded.

Diaper rash giving you trouble? she asked.

Jared started to laugh and Lee made this laughing snort, but both of them capped their laughter before Ryan could give them dagger eyes. He gave Lucy the dagger eyes instead. He pinned her to the sidewalk with daggers.

A kiss on your ass won't help. Lucy grinned. **What you need is baby powder.**

Jared and Lee plugged their laughter but a little still leaked out. Ryan turned and glared. For a split second I was worried for them, but only for a second. Gluing their hips to Ryan's was their choice.

Ryan looked back at Lucy. She was smiling, flashing her gravel teeth. Owen stepped forward and pulled her hat off. I think I gasped when I saw the brick-wall welt on her forehead.

Someone try to knock some sense into you? Ryan said.

Owen laughed a half laugh. Lucy grabbed the hat back and shook it at Owen. **You like being one of his sheep, following Little Bo Peep wherever he goes?**

Med moved forward. **Who're you calling sheep?**

You have any idea how ugly you are? Ryan said. **You have the face of a —**

He **likes what he sees.** Lucy cut him off as she nodded toward me. **He's been taking my picture.**

Ryan smirked. **In case you haven't noticed, your boyfriend looks like a lemon-sucking monkey.**

Jared and Med nodded. Owen looked at Lucy and said, **Takes one to know one.**

Lucy shook her head and bent down to pick up her coffee cup. **You got no guts, any of you. Pickin' on him. Pickin' on me.** She shook the empty cup at Ryan. **We're easy pickings.** She plucked a coin and dropped it into her cup. **You're gutless.**

She picked up a few more coins, one at a time. It's like she was making a point with each dropped coin. I bent down and handed her a few she had missed.

She stood up.

Probably can't spell "gutless," right?

I knew Lucy was asking a rhetorical question, which is a question-that-isn't-really-a-question because you don't expect an answer. It's another way of making a point. But Lee looked at Lucy and said, **G-U-T.** He stopped for a second. **L-A-S-S.**

Lucy started to laugh. It was a quiet laugh, like she was remembering a good joke she didn't want to share. When she finished picking up all the coins, she shook her cup at Ryan. The coins rattled.

Gutless, she said again.

Ryan didn't say anything. Neither did anyone else. Owen looked like he was itching to talk but wouldn't until Ryan gave him the nod.

I waited for something to happen.

A minute passed. Ryan stared at Lucy. She stared back at him.

Then Ryan walked away.

Med and Jared stood there like they were in a play and had forgotten their lines. Then they left. Owen and Lee followed.

I noticed one more coin on the sidewalk and picked it up.

Lucy looked at me. **Keep it.**

I curled my fingers around the coin. **Are you okay?**

She snorted. **Little Bo Peep's got nothing on Husband Number Two. Now he was a handful.**

You were married?

The words slipped out before I could stop them. It was the first and only time I heard Lucy mention a husband. I didn't want her to think that Wedding Day Lucy sounded as impossible as Astronaut Lucy to me.

She held up three fingers. **Three times. What about yourself?**

Engaged.

Lucy raised her eyebrows. **Where's your engagement ring?**

I picked up an old twist tie from the sidewalk and wrapped it around my finger.

Lucy smiled at me and said, **Lucky girl.**

When I got home, my father was in the kitchen, making supper. He was using lots of spices, so I could tell I wouldn't like it. About once a month my father gets it into his head that he's going to Introduce Us to Something Foreign, as if the dish was a new kid at school who didn't speak a word of English. You had to be polite and smile a lot.

Hope you're hungry, he said.

I had no appetite after watching Ryan get into Lucy's face. But I didn't want to make my father feel bad, so I avoided the answer by asking a question.

What are you making?

He tried to pronounce something in Italian, but by the time he was through I knew even an Italian would have asked for subtitles.

I'd been meaning to ask you about that. He pointed to the kitchen table where I had left the Diane Arbus book that morning. **Where did you find that?**

I told him I got it at the library.

We still need libraries? he asked.

I tried to swallow a sigh, but part of it leaked out. My father sees everything in black-and-white, without a heck of a lot of room for any shades in between. For him the invention of e-books means *libraries should be mothballed.* He says *women shouldn't be firefighters, end of story.* As far as he's concerned, *we shouldn't tamper with the names we're given,* so *it's flat-out wrong* for a Susan to call herself Suzin. We get into arguments where I try to mix in different shades with his black-and-whiteness, but I end up with a lot more sighs than shades.

When my mother came home, my father showed her the Diane Arbus book. I heard her say, **What do you make of it?** but I didn't hear what my father said. It was a grunt and a mumble. (Maybe that's how they came up with the word "grumble.")

I went up to my room. I was putting together a Lucy section on one of my walls and had to make space for it. I placed the Lucy photographs beside the *Great Escape*, a bunch of pictures of fire escapes. In one picture a kid is sitting on a fire escape, holding a purse.

Take whatever you want.

He pointed to the step beneath his feet.

When I think about taking the photograph I remember what I didn't take. The hairbrush. The lipstick. The leprechaun key ring. The pair of sunglasses. The pen. The tube of hand lotion. The container filled with blue pills. They were all laid out neatly on the step, as if they were on display.

I told the boy the only thing I wanted to take was his picture.

He looked disappointed and annoyed. He turned both ways to see if there were any other customers.

Then take it.

If a picture is worth a thousand words, those thousand words keep changing. Sometimes the words are about a kid with a purse (you can't tell if he stole it or found it). Sometimes the words are about a purseless woman. Sometimes the words are about the person taking the picture, and what he left behind on an unseen step.

I called the picture *Boy Holding Purse*.

I've seen pictures with titles that made no sense, real head-scratching titles that gave your fingers a scratch workout. Like a picture of a cow in front of a barn, and instead of calling it *Cow in Front of a Barn* it was called *Intersection*.

Diane Arbus wasn't like that. She gave her pictures normal titles, like *Puerto Rican Woman with a Beauty Mark, NYC, 1965* or *King and Queen of Senior Citizens Dance, NYC, 1970*, which is a picture of two old coots, sitting on plain chairs, wearing crowns and long capes.

A normal title describes what you see. But you would need a title that stretches from Australia to Zagreb to describe everything beyond the picture. This is one reason why I have this so-called obsession with photography. Since you can never get the whole picture, you should wonder about the part of the picture you can't see. If you ask me, there are not enough *What the heck?* photographs around.

My mother walked up to my closed door and said, **Supper's ready.** And then she said, **Do I have to remind you to wash your hands?** which is her way of reminding me but pretending it's not a reminder because she hasn't officially reminded me.

At the table, I wished Watson was around so I could give him my portion of my father's new foreign dish. But there was no Watson, so I poked at my plate and ate just enough that my father would think I liked it but not so much that he would think I wanted more. When my mother asked how my day was, I didn't tell her about Lucy and Ryan. I just said, **Good**, and she said, **That's what you always say, sweetheart**.

No one said a heck of a lot else for the rest of the meal, which was fine by me.

Dessert was fruit salad, which shouldn't be called dessert because everything in it once hung on a tree. Which means it's boring. Which means I said, **May I please be excused?** without taking a bite.

After dinner I called Sean. I told him about my latest run-in with The Problem. I described how Lucy called Ryan gutless and how he just stood there and didn't say a word.

Ryan? Sean said. **Speechless?**

I described the strolling strollers. **I wonder what Ryan would have said or done to Lucy if there was no one around to see him do it.**

Sean didn't say anything. He didn't have to. When you're in the same boat as someone else, you can say things without saying them and the other person in the boat knows exactly what you mean.

Now we're going to have to wait for something to happen. He tried to sound like one of the cigarette-smoking, Scotch-on-the-rocks detectives he loves. **I don't want to spend time in that waiting room.**

Sometimes Sean gets too caught up in his hard-boiled detective talk but I don't say anything. Sometimes, being in the same boat also means taking something you want to say and tossing it overboard before the other person in the boat notices.

Did you understand that poem Mr. Binsley handed out? I asked.

I had decided to talk about something else. Anything else.

I didn't want to spend any more time thinking about that waiting room.

Something was bugging Lucy. There was no empty coffee cup by her crate. She hadn't made a new sign. A bunch of old ones were lying flat on the sidewalk. *Civil War Vet. Saving for Retirement. Free Wi-Fi.*

So no new Lucy signs. No fresh Lucy laughter. Just Lucy looking like she was chewing on some bitter candy. It reminded me of one the photographs I had taken of her, where her eyes are like knobs on a drawer. If you pulled the drawer open, you could see what was happening inside Lucy's head, but she wasn't having any of that. The drawer was locked tight. I sat down beside her.

What was Kenya like?

I thought a question might open the drawer, but Lucy looked at me as if I had not only a scar on my cheek but a slug at the end of it.

Kenya. You told me you've been to Kenya. Twice.

Another long look, as if the slug was now dancing on my nose.

Can't remember.

I didn't think Lucy had made up going to Kenya, but I didn't think that was the whole story either. I figured I'd have as many lines on my face as Lucy by the time I got the almost-whole story. It wouldn't be the whole story because everybody keeps a slice. One photographer in *Cameras and Conversations* says that every photograph is a slice of life and *You never know what slice you'll be served* when you take a picture. If you ask me, the best pictures make you want a second slice when you don't even know what the heck it was you ate in the first place.

I had brought a copy of *Lucy Dancing in the Lane* to show to her. Lucy chewed on it like she was two days away from the last bite.

I've never been to Vegas, she said. It sounded like an apology. I tilted my head.

The day you took these pictures, I told you I'd been a show-girl in Sin City. She held up the photograph to her face the way I've seen women holding up mirrors when they put on makeup. Straight on and real close. **Never so much as dipped my baby toe in it.**

Lucy put the photo down and stared off in the distance. Then she took my hand and wrapped her fingers around it. She held it like that for about a minute before she unwrapped it and gave it back.

It didn't feel right. It didn't feel wrong. It felt like something she had to do.

What about Kenya? I asked.

What about it?

Have you ever been there?

Lucy looked over my shoulder, as if Kenya was a few feet behind me.

I can't remember. She stared at the toes that never made it to Vegas. **I think so.**

She gave me another long, hard look. She wasn't just reading my eyes. It's like my face was a book and she was deciding which chapter to start with. She touched the spot on her neck and the side of her ear where my scars would have been on her.

What happened?

Usually I don't tell people what happened. But I had a feeling I could tell Lucy anything and she wouldn't answer with an oversize laugh: the bigger the laugh, the smaller you feel. So I told her about the time when I was six years old and wanted a spoonful of alphabet soup. I took two big spoons because I wanted to spell *Tyrannosaurus rex*. The two-spoon word was going to be a surprise for my parents.

The surprise was on me.

So were the flames.

The soup pot was at the back of the stove. I was too busy looking for a *Y* and an *X* to notice the pot of applesauce on the front burner. I don't remember a heck of a lot about what happened, but I remember my mother screaming and my father wrapping me in a towel. And I remember the smell. It's a smell you can never describe and never forget.

Lucy was quiet for a long time before she finally spoke.

Too bad you were such a wicked speller.

I didn't know what she was talking about.

I'm talkin' What If. What if all you wanted was to spell "cat"? You might've been in and outta there in no time.

I thought about what Lucy had just said. I thought of six-year-old me scooping three letters instead of fishing for sixteen. How things might have turned out differently.

"Cat" could've saved your ass. She smiled a gravel smile.

I smiled back at Lucy. **It's not my ass that got burned.**

We both cracked up. When Lucy starting saying **Here, kitty, kitty!** I laughed even more. Some people stopped and tried to figure us out. They looked for a cat that wasn't there, then kept walking.

The laughter faded, but not the feeling that came with it.

I know what I'm talkin' about, Lucy said at last. **I've spent a lot of time wondering What If.**

We were quiet for a few minutes. I had a feeling we were both thinking about What Ifs.

Lucy bent over and picked up *Lucy Dancing in the Lane.*

Can I keep this?

I nodded.

When I walked away, she was holding on to my photograph with both hands, and I was holding on to her laughter.

This picture also Made a Difference.

Ms. Karamath showed me a photograph of a boy and girl running. The boy is a teenager. He's carrying a younger boy in his arms. All three of them are black.

Is the boy in his arms dead?

Ms. Karamath nodded. She told me the kid who was being carried was Hector Pieterson, and that the picture was taken in Soweto, South Africa, in 1976. The black students didn't want to speak Afrikaans at school, which was the language some white South Africans spoke, and these white people made the rules even though there were a lot more blacks than whites.

Rules are made to be broken, I said.

Ms. Karamath nodded. **Some rules are unfair, T—. Break them and you must gird yourself for more unfairness.**

Hector was shot by police for participating in a political protest. The boy carrying him is the picture of grief. The girl has her eyes closed and one hand open wide like she's saying *Stop!* only she's running. My guess is she's running from the Rule Makers before another Rule Breaker gets shot. I wanted to ask Ms. Karamath who made the Rule Makers rule makers in the first place, but I knew she would say, *It's complicated*, which is what my parents say a thousand times a month, as if the whole planet is a Rubik's Cube and no one has the time to figure it out.

Ms. Karamath stepped away to help someone else. I studied the picture for a few minutes, then walked over to her.

Unspeakable.

Ms. Karamath looked at me.

The name of this picture. I call it *Unspeakable* because it looks like the boy and girl are so upset, they can't speak.

Ms. Karamath didn't say a word for about five years.

Very good, T—. That's very good.

I told her that's not what Diane Arbus would probably have called it and she said that was okay because I wasn't Diane Arbus. She looked at the picture and kept nodding her head and saying, *Unspeakable.* She told me that "unspeakable" is also a synonym for "terrible." Then she said my title was **ironic** because the picture **spoke volumes.**

This time I asked her what "ironic" meant, because I didn't want to spend all that time with irony but no definition.

Opposites, Ms. Karamath said. **That's the best way I can explain it. Picture a crowd-pleasing clown who makes people laugh but celebrates his birthday without a single friend or so much as a slice of cake. That would be ironic.**

I tried to think of other examples of irony, like a mapmaker with a lousy sense of direction or a florist with a dead-grass front yard. I asked Ms..Karamath if I could have the copy of *Unspeakable.*

My pleasure, she said. And she wasn't being ironic.

I was in my room in the Vault, arranging the photographs I had taken of Lucy before her run-in with Ryan, when I heard some laughter from the alley behind the building.

It was Ryan's laughter.

It's not domino laughter that moves like falling tiles, down one row, up the next. Ryan's laughter starts and stops with Ryan. Jared and Med are just his echoes.

I walked toward a hole in the wall that used to be a window and looked out. Joined at the Hip were standing in a circle, laughing. In the middle of the circle was Lucy.

She was on the ground. She wasn't laughing. It looked like she was covered with flour. Her hair, her face, her coat. Ryan was holding a plastic bottle over her and shaking flour out the way you shake salt on bland potatoes. He kept shaking and shaking it.

Diaper rash giving you trouble? Ryan said.

The penny dropped. Lucy wasn't covered with flour. It was baby powder.

I started taking pictures. Sometimes, a camera is a different kind of witness. It can say a heck of a lot without saying a word.

Ryan smiled. Med smiled too. Jared's smile was about a block away before it showed up, and it didn't look like it wanted to stay when it finally got there.

Gutless, Lucy said.

Ryan stopped shaking. He handed the bottle of baby powder to Jared.

What'd you say?

Lucy looked up at Ryan. Her face was very dusty and very white.

Gutless, Lucy said. **Three of you. One of me.**

She coughed this watery cough and looked straight at Jared, waiting for him to shake the bottle.

No one said anything. I could hear myself breathing.

Then Ryan smacked Lucy on the side of the head.

Why'd you do that? Jared asked.

Ryan told him to **Shut up!** He hit Lucy again.

I wanted to say something but nothing came out. I reached into my backpack for my cell phone to call 911, but the more I dug, the more my heart sank. My mother had taken my cell phone to get the glass replaced. It had shattered after I fell on the sidewalk. Tripped by Joined at the Hip.

When Ryan struck Lucy again, I took a picture, proof of what happens when a psychopath goes psycho. Lucy took a swat at Ryan and he swatted back.

Then Lucy toppled over. Ryan kicked her like she was stuck to the ground and he was testing the glue. Med joined in. I felt frozen. I didn't know what to do.

Jared said, **Let's go, let's go, let's go!**

Ryan grabbed a fistful of Lucy's hair, yanked her head back, and pulled something out of his back pocket.

No! I shouted.

Everyone looked up. Ryan. Med. Jared. Lucy.

I saw them looking at me, holding my camera and holding my breath.

Ryan was live-wire shocked. That lasted about two seconds before he changed into a Ryan I had never seen before. Everything had been squeezed out of him except his anger.

Lucy moaned. I could hear my heart pounding in my ears. Ryan slipped the something into his back pocket and ran toward the Vault. I knew my goose was cooked.

But first they had to catch the goose.

I turned around and ran. Maybe I could be a diversion. If Joined at the Hip were busy chasing after me, Lucy would have the chance to get away.

You're dead meat! Ryan yelled.

I ran up some stairs to the third floor. I tripped and banged my teeth. The taste of blood filled my mouth but I kept running. Joined at the Hip were getting closer. I couldn't make out the words but I knew they were speaking Angry.

On the fourth floor I saw a closet filled with old wires. I stepped inside and closed the door. The wires felt like cobwebs. My heart was beating so quickly I thought it would pop out and fly away.

I heard footsteps coming up the second-floor stairs.

I closed my eyes. I clutched my camera. I heard the drip-drip of a leak nearby. I licked my teeth. My mouth wasn't bleeding anymore.

They were on the third floor now.

How many pictures do you think he got? Jared asked.

Doesn't matter, Ryan said. **No one's going to see them.** His voice sounded deep-water cold.

I heard the sound of metal clanging, then loud voices. Joined at the Hip didn't know what it was but I recognized them. Some days the homeless people who lived in the building got into big arguments, duking it out with shopping carts instead of fists. On those days I avoided the Vault.

You woke me up! a voice boomed out of nowhere, too near to be a part of the shopping cart fight below. It was a third-floor voice, very close and very angry. **You're stepping on my rug!**

What rug? Jared said.

Watch your step! Rug Man sounded tall.

Med said, **He has a metal bar. . . .**

The next thing I heard were feet running down stairs. Heavy footsteps pounded after them a minute later, then faded.

I waited about five weeks before I cracked open the closet door. No sign of Joined at the Hip or Rug Man.

I walked to another hole that used to be a window. I poked my head through.

Lucy was gone.

I walked around the outside of the Vault about a hundred times. I didn't think Lucy could have gone very far because of the way she had been kicked. She must have had bruises and maybe even some broken bones. I was going to yell *Lucy!* but that sounded like I was looking for a lost dog. I knew I had to find her before Joined at the Hip found me.

I went down alleys and up laneways. I checked under fire escapes. I looked behind those big-enough-to-hide-a-body garbage bins. I even tried the Linden Parkette. I knew she wouldn't be sliding down the slide but I thought I might see her catching her breath.

There were three kids in the sandbox but no breath-catching Lucy.

I left the parkette and walked around a corner.

Lucy!

Her name jumped out of my mouth as I walked around a corner.

She was way down the block.

She was walking with a limp.

I called her name again as I ran to catch up with her.

But she wasn't Lucy. She was wearing a Lucy coat and a Lucy hat but that's where the Lucy ended.

Let go of me! the woman said.

I didn't realize I had grabbed her arm.

You're not Lucy, I said.

She pulled her arm away. **I'm late, is what I am.**

She limped away. I went up and down about ten more streets. It was getting dark. I was feeling discouraged. Dark and discouraged aren't a good combination, so I went home.

When I stepped through the door my mother said, **You look wan.**

I told her I was feeling okay and went straight to my room. I sat on my bed and looked at all the pictures I had taken of Lucy and Joined at the Hip. There were twenty-seven in total. By the fifth picture my insides had turned to soup. By the tenth my bones were noodles. By the time I got to the last picture I was on the floor. I didn't think I would ever get up.

In one picture Med is kicking Lucy. She has an *Ooof!* look. It's like Med had kicked something out of her that had been there for so long she had forgotten it even existed. She looks shocked and wounded at the same time.

In one shot of Jared, his eyes don't look like eyes. He's not looking at Lucy. He's not looking at Ryan or Med. He's looking at something that isn't there. And whatever that unsomething is, he doesn't know what to do with it.

Lucy has her hands over her ears in one image, like a kid who doesn't want to hear something a parent is saying. In another she's swatting Ryan and he's swatting her back. Only their swats happened at the same time, so their hands are joined together and it looks like they're dancing. Photographs capture a single moment but sometimes you need side-by-side moments to make sense of them.

After I moved all the photographs onto a memory stick, I deleted them from my camera and laptop. I hung the stick around my neck like a dog tag and wore it to bed.

I wondered where Lucy was sleeping. If she was sleeping. If there was any *Ooof!* left in her, wherever she was. If she thought I was gutless.

Suddenly I felt very, very tired.

My eyes were closed but that didn't stop the pictures from getting in.

I lay in bed the next morning and thought about Lucy.

Did she collapse into a bruised heap on the street?

Did people walk by? Did anyone help her?

Did she curl up on one of her cardboard signs?

I pictured Lucy, leaning against a wall, beaten and bruised, with not enough Lucy left in her to fill a coffee cup.

I wondered what Joined at the Hip were going to do to me. I knew they were going to do something. I kept thinking of Ryan's smile. Sometimes, smiles are worse than snarls. You know what you're getting when you're given a snarl. But a smile can be like wrapping paper. It doesn't tell you anything about what's inside.

I was sitting at the kitchen table when my mother said, **Oh dear.**

I was supposed to be eating breakfast but I had lost my appetite and didn't know if I would ever find it again. My mother took a sip of her coffee.

Oh my.

My father looked at my mother. She kept reading her newspaper and saying things like **This is too much.**

My father finally said, **What?**

This woman.

My father took a loud sip of his coffee. **Which woman?**

A homeless woman died just a few blocks over. Last night. Not ten minutes from here. My mother mentioned the Linden

Parkette. She looked at the kitchen wall as if it suddenly had a window. **A dog walker found her beneath a slide.**

The same slide Lucy went down a hundred times.

They think she may have choked on her own vomit.

My father had one ear in the conversation and both eyes on a text message. **Those people should be locked up at night.**

I bit my lip.

For their own good. And ours.

When I heard my mother say **baby powder**, I felt something crack inside me.

I asked if I could be excused. They didn't hear me, or each other.

I went to my room and sat on my bed. I felt emptier than a thousand empty coffee cups. I had never known anyone who died, other than a grandfather who I barely remember. I didn't know Lucy all that well, but the parts I knew I really liked. There were other parts to her I would never see because she was gone. When someone goes, they take all the missing parts with them. Maybe that's one reason why we miss them so much.

Ms. Karamath gave me three binders.

Each one has a label.

Binder No. 2 and Binder No. 3 are empty.

This is Binder No. 1.

Binder No. 1 has photographs of Lucy and her signs. Lucy dancing. Lucy eating strawberries. Lucy on a slide.

But there are no photographs of Lucy's Last Moments in the binder. When you look at a Last Moment photograph, you get the wrong picture. You see a Lucy who is small and broken, who doesn't look like much more than a pile of old, toss-it clothing. Ryan has the upper hand, so he leaves a bigger impression than lower-hand Lucy.

Some photographs are louder than other photographs. They're the ones that get all the attention even if there are a thousand others that have something to say.

If Lucy's Last Moments are in a binder, then the other Lucy photographs will never be heard.

Some days those moments are so loud I have to cover my ears.

By the time I got to school I had thrown up twice. I gargled with chocolate milk that I bought at McCreary's Will-Never-Be-a-Corner Store. I had to get a late slip from Mrs. Quan in the office.

I knew I would have to wait until lunch before I could speak with Sean. I wanted to talk to him about what to do with *Lucy's Last Moments*. Sometimes the distance between first period and lunch feels so long you might as well pack a sandwich to eat before you get there.

But as soon as I sat down beside Sean in the cafeteria, Ryan sat down on my other side.

Let's play a game.

Med and Jared sat down across from me. If you didn't know any better, you would think the five of us were old friends. I knew better. So did Sean.

You finished eating? Med asked.

I hadn't even started. The appetite I had lost at breakfast still hadn't shown up.

It looks like it may rain, said Ryan. **It's a perfect day for indoor games.**

I looked outside. The sun was shining. The sky was blue.

A perfect day for indoor games, Med repeated.

Ryan leaned forward on the cafeteria table so he could look at Sean. **You can't play, Tonto.** Joined at the Hip like to come up with different sidekick names for Sean. **This is a game one person plays at a time.**

And it's really simple, Med said.

Super simple, Ryan said. **All you have to do is look at a picture and tell us what it is. If you get it right, you get a point. Once you get three points, you win. Easy, right?**

I nod.

You ready? Jared asked.

No, I unsaid.

Let's start, Ryan said. He nodded at Jared, who pulled out a picture of a knife.

What's this?

I looked at the picture. I looked at Sean. He was wearing a *What the heck?* look. Ryan punched me gently in the shoulder.

Don't look at your girlfriend.

Med smirked.

Look at the picture.

I stared at the picture.

What is it?

A knife.

Ryan shook his head, like I had just told him it was a watermelon. **It's not a knife.** He looked at Med and Jared. **Do you see a knife?**

Med and Jared shook their heads. Ryan said, **They don't see a knife.**

I looked back at the picture of the knife. **A utensil**, I said.

Ryan took the picture out of Jared's hand and brought it toward me.

This isn't a knife. This isn't a utensil. He held up the picture. **This is a picture of a knife.** He looked at Med and Jared, who were both smiling. **Do you see a knife?**

They shook their heads.

I bet if we asked sweet Sean over here what he sees, he'd say the same thing.

Sean didn't say a word.

Ryan jabbed me with the picture. **Does that hurt?**

I shook my head.

'Course not. Because it's not a knife. So for one point, tell me what you see.

I looked at the picture of the knife and said, **A not-knife.**

Ryan laughed and slapped me on the back.

A "not-knife." I like that. One point.

Med took out a picture of a camera.

What do you see? Ryan asked.

I looked at the picture of the camera for a long time. I looked at Sean.

A not-camera.

Ryan did a very lame job of showing he was surprised. He raised his eyebrows and opened his eyes so they were as big as saucers.

Really?

I didn't reply. I knew whatever I said would be wrong.

Ryan looked at the picture. **I don't know what your problem is. I see a camera.** He showed the picture to Med and Jared. **Do you see a camera?**

Med and Jared nodded.

You already have one point, Tinker Bell. There's still time to get another. Ryan pointed to the picture. **What do you see?**

I looked at the lunch lady, who was scraping a piece of gum off a table. I looked at the picture.

A camera.

Ryan clapped. Then Med and Jared clapped. Other kids looked at us. The lunch lady stopped scrubbing and looked at us too. She shook her head. She thought we were playing some kind of game with rules adults will never understand.

Half a point, Ryan said.

Half a point? Even though I didn't understand the crazy game, I didn't get why I didn't receive a full point.

For the rest of the point, you have to tell us if there are any pictures in the camera.

I waited about half a second before I said, **No pictures.** *Deleted but saved*, I unsaid.

Ryan nodded. **There are no pictures in it.** He stopped and looked at Med and Jared. **No pictures, right.**

I looked at Ryan. **No pictures.**

He smiled and slapped me twice on the back. **Two points. One more and you win.**

Jared took out a picture of a match. **What do we have here?**

I stared at the picture. **A match.**

Ryan pretended to be disappointed again. **It's not a match**, he said. **Look carefully.**

I pretended to look carefully. **All I see is a match.**

You're one point away from winning, so I'm going to give you another chance.

I looked at Sean. All he did was shrug. There wasn't a heck of a lot I could do with a shrug.

A wooden match, I said.

Ryan tried to look concerned, but the only thing Ryan ever cares about is Ryan.

Here's a clue. Because I like you. He slapped me on the back like we were old buddies. **What do you get when you strike a match? A flame.**

Ryan shook his head. **And a whole bunch of flames make a . . . A fire.**

Ryan put the picture of the match down. His face changed. It was like the lunch lady had wiped every fake smile and grin away and all that was left was the real Ryan. If he was a Diane Arbus photograph, he would have been called *Angry Boy.*

You know what happens when you play with fire?

I leaned back. **You get burned.**

You get very burned. But you don't have anything to worry about because there are no pictures. Isn't that right?

Ryan looked at Jared and Med. They nodded.

You'll be careful around matches because matches turn to fire and fire can burn you. He stopped. **Again. And badly.**

Very badly, said Med.

We don't want you to get hurt, said Jared.

Ryan shook his head. He gathered all the pictures and stood up. **The last thing we want is for you to get hurt.**

Ryan walked away and Jared and Med followed him like puppies.

Looks like the game is over, Sean said when they were gone.

It just started, I said.

On the way home after school that day I told Sean what had happened to Lucy in the alley. I told him about the baby powder and how she had called Joined at the Hip gutless again, how that one word detonated something inside Ryan, how Joined at the Hip chased after me after my **No!** I described my block-by-block search for Lucy that went nowhere.

Sean didn't speak for about five minutes after I finished describing *Lucy's Last Moments.*

Where did you put the dog tag?

I pulled it out from under my shirt.

Take it to the police.

I thought about that, I told him. **For about ten seconds. I** reminded him what Ryan had told Sergeant Chomack. **I'm in their system. He'll tell them this crazy homeless lady attacked him and all I did was stand back and take pictures.**

Then tell your parents, Sean said.

I slipped the dog tag back beneath my shirt.

There's no point.

One look at *Lucy's Last Moments* and my mother would blame me for not helping Ryan as he fought off a lunatic. Then she'd blame herself for the burns that made me into a don't-just-stand-there bystander. As for my black-and-white father, a model student like Ryan can never do wrong, so my story couldn't have been right. With

Sergeant Chomack and Bubbles Bianco in his corner, Ryan's word would be taken over mine. I was cornerless.

This isn't a make-believe murder mystery where everything gets wrapped up by the last page, I said. **There is no last page with Ryan. If he was locked up, he would still call the shots. When he says, "Cut!," Owen will say "How deep?"**

We spoke Silent for half a block. The look on Sean's face said how sorry he was for the bind I was in. I made an in-my-head list of other adults I could speak to. There was only one I thought would actually hear what I had to say.

Maybe I could talk to Ms. Karamath, I said.

Sean stopped walking. **Ms. Karamath doesn't have the power to stop them. And they have to be stopped, T—. Look at what they did to Lucy.**

I told Sean it wasn't about power.

What's it about?

Getting the truth out, I said.

Ryan was smooth-talking and he had smooth-talking parents who knew the kind of people who could smooth things over. Ms. Karamath wasn't like that. She knew the truth could be bumpy and uncomfortable.

Ms. Karamath understands me.

I didn't get how that worked and I still don't. Sometimes you can feel old-sweatshirt comfortable with someone you've just met and two-left-shoes awkward with people you've known for ages.

Sean's eyes were soft and sharp at the same time. **Be careful, T—.**

I nodded. I thought about *Lucy's Last Moments* and how messy things had become. I wanted to clean up the mess. I wasn't sure how. I knew Sean was right. The mess would keep spreading, like those huge oil spills that turn blue water black and leave birds so covered with oil they never fly again.

I didn't want to be that flightless bird.

It's for you.

My mother covered the mouthpiece with one hand so whoever was on the phone wouldn't hear what she was about to say.

It's not Sean.

She was smiling but trying not to smile. She knew Sean was my only friend and she kept hoping I'd make new ones, as if friends were something you make out of wood and glue.

I think it's Ryan, she whispered. She handed me the phone as if the Pope was on the other end.

Hello?

I didn't hear anything.

Hello?

I figured it was a prank call. I was about to hang up when someone spoke.

Your cell phone isn't on.

I told Ryan the glass shattered when he tripped me and I fell on the sidewalk.

Sorry, he said. Ryan is so used to artificial apologies he would never recognize the taste of a real one. **Let's meet.**

My mouth went dry. The last thing in the world I wanted to do was meet with Joined at the Hip. I told them everything they wanted to hear in the cafeteria game. Why did they want a rematch?

Why?

Never mind "why." Ask me where.

I asked him where.

He mentioned a corner about five blocks away. He told me to be there in ten minutes.

I told him I needed fifteen.

Don't make it twenty.

I thought I heard Ryan laugh before he hung up.

I wondered for about a nanosecond what would happen if I didn't show up. It wouldn't make a difference. Whatever Ryan was going to do to me he would do another time instead. It's not like evil people are stamped with an expiration date. They're old-milk sour from day one, and they stay that way forever.

I told my mother I was going out to buy some gum. She told me to make sure the gum was sugarless and then asked who was on the phone. I told her it was **no one** and she smiled and said, **He didn't sound like a no one to me.** When I told her it wasn't Ryan but someone from my class asking about homework, all she said was, **Oh.** If disappointment was a perfume, my mother would have bottles of the stuff.

Before I left the house, I took off my dog tag and put it inside my sock drawer. I left my camera at home too. The five blocks from where I live to where I-didn't-know-what-was-going-to-happen were way shorter than I ever thought they were. I tried to find ways to stretch things out. I tied my shoe. I did buy some gum. I looked inside store windows I never cared about before and stared as if there were doughnuts inside instead of boring tiles or pictures of women with hairdos from a thousand years ago. I offered to help an old man cross the street but he got all huffy and said, **I can do it myself.** I waited a few minutes to see if there was anyone else I could assist. All

I saw were two teenagers kissing like crazy and I could tell they didn't need an extra hand.

I could see Ryan standing on the corner as I got closer. Jared and Med weren't around. Neither was anyone else from his crew. Little Bo Peep must have given his sheep the night off.

Good to see you, Ryan said. He smiled. I wasn't sure why he wanted to meet on a street corner. What could he do to me if a million people were watching?

Let's go.

I didn't move. **Where?**

Never mind where.

I did mind "where," but there was no point in saying a word if your words are like snowflakes in July.

Ryan started walking. I walked behind him. Five blocks later we were back where I had started from, standing in front of my house. He looked at it like he had grown up there, all big smiles and *Remember the time?* nods.

Funny, Ryan said. **We live in the same neighborhood but we're not exactly neighbors, are we?**

I shrugged.

How long before you invite me in?

Another shrug. I wondered how many shrugs I would shrug before this would be over.

I want to be able to walk in any old time. That's what good neighbors do, right? They watch out for each other. They have a key to each other's houses.

He walked around the house like a housepainter deciding what color goes where, stopping to run his hand along the windowsills.

111

Thing is, I don't need a key.

We were standing in the backyard. I could see my mother in the kitchen, grating carrots.

Ryan pointed to a bedroom window. **I could invite myself in any time of day. Or night.** He smiled. **You ready to play for five bonus points?**

I didn't know what he was talking about.

He took out a picture of a muzzle.

What do you see? Ryan asked.

We played this game yesterday, I said. **I'm not playing again.**

His smile vanished. **I make the rules, not you. Besides, this won't take long. Five minutes and then you can call your girlfriend.**

Everything in me stiffened. **Leave Sean out of this.**

He was never in. Ryan tilted his head. **But now that I think about it . . .**

I didn't want him to think about it, so I looked at the picture. **A muzzle,** I said.

Very good. He was enjoying the game. **Know what happens when a muzzle doesn't do the trick?**

My mother wiped her forehead, then got back to more grating. I scratched my chest. I could feel the leathery scars beneath my fingers.

You don't teach the dog new tricks. You teach the dog a permanent lesson.

I could hear myself breathing. **I'm not afraid of you**, I lied.

Afraid? Ryan said it twice, then rested his elbow on my shoulder.

This is a safe neighborhood. He leaned in and talked in a back-of-the-class-whisper. **Until a dog barks.**

Ryan started to walk away, then turned around.

Sleep well, he said. **Your parents too.**

He didn't look back again. All I could think about was what lay ahead.

After a restless night, I got to school early. As I walked toward the main doors, Bubbles Bianco waved me over.

What brings you here at this hour? He smiled. **You're not a worm catcher, are you?**

Some kids on the basketball team were there for an early practice. Mr. Ramshaw calls them worm catchers because early birds catch worms. According to Mr. Ramshaw, we have to decide right now if we're going to be worm catchers or worms because *the choices you make in grade seven will follow you until you're seventy.* Ryan and his crew are all early birds.

I held up my camera and explained I was there to take a picture of a display Ms. Karamath had put together. Ms. Karamath had told me our conversations about photographs that Made a Difference inspired her to create a wall of iconic photographs. I thought it would be interesting to try and squeeze as much icon as I could into a single photograph.

Is that right? Bubbles Bianco said.

I repeated the same words Ms. Karamath said to me. **Sometimes, a photographer is there to capture a moment in history.** I used the example she gave. **Like when Jack Ruby shot Lee Harvey Oswald.**

Bubbles Bianco frowned. **What else do you do with that camera?**

I shrugged. **I like taking pictures of people.**

His frown shriveled into a grimace. **What kind of people?**

Whoever catches my fancy, I said. It was an answer I thought Bubbles Bianco would like.

Your fancy, he said. The way he said it I could tell he was about to give me a lecture. **I see.**

He took my camera from me and turned it over in his hands, as if it came with a key he didn't have for a keyhole he couldn't find. He bubbled for about five minutes before I understood what he was getting at.

Privacy, he was saying. **You take a picture of me now, how soon before it's seen by someone in Kuala Lumpur?** He tried snapping his fingers but he was all fingers and no snap. **Seconds, young man. Seconds.**

I didn't know where Kuala Lumpur was but I couldn't imagine why a Lumpurian would want a picture of Bubbles Bianco.

My question to you is, what if I don't want my picture shown in Malaysia? Or anywhere else? He said students taking photographs of students in **compromising positions** was getting out of control. He repeated the word **privacy** about a hundred times. Then he tossed in **violation** and stirred it with some other words — **invasion, humiliation, boundaries** — until he was in a bubbly lather.

I told him I only took photographs of people who knew they were being photographed. I could tell he didn't fancy my fancy.

I heard a low murmur and looked up. Lee and Owen stood at the end of the hall, watching us. When they saw I had seen them, they turned and went down the hallway.

Bubbles Bianco told me to **exercise caution** and handed my camera back to me. **I suggest you keep that thing on a very tight leash. Understood?**

I understood. My camera was a dog he wanted muzzled.

First I heard a bounce. Then I felt the ball.

I turned around. Owen's eyes were all flames. The basketball had bounced off my back and into Lee's hands.

You don't look well, Owen said.

Lee nodded. **Looks like you could use a trip to the bathroom.**

Owen grabbed one arm. Lee grabbed the other. After the bathroom door closed behind us, Owen shoved me against a wall.

What did you tell him? Owen asked.

Who?

He stepped forward, closing the gap between us. **Bianco. We saw you talking to him.**

They must have seen Bianco giving my camera the once-over and jumped to the wrong conclusion. They thought I was showing him what Joined at the Hip had done to Lucy.

I didn't say anything. I told them about Bianco's bubbling about privacy.

Owen said I was **a lousy liar.** He must be used to only the best-tasting lies. **Know what I'm thinking? I think we should see if your head fits into a toilet bowl. What do you think, Lee?**

Lee grinned. **I once read that drowning doesn't take more than a few inches of water.**

I was surprised Lee could read. I knew he couldn't spell "gutless."

Twinkle, Twinkle, Little Scar has a big head, Owen said. **Let's try it out.**

Owen sounded so much like Ryan I was beginning to think they were in the same boat. Only their boat was a toxic-waste barge. Lee had just grabbed my arm when a toilet flushed.

Jared stepped out of a stall. He looked at me for a split second but it was enough of a split to see a flicker. I wasn't sure what kind of flicker it was but better a flicker than a fuse.

What are you doing?

I knew it wasn't the question Owen and Lee were expecting to hear. Jared didn't wait for them to answer.

Do you know what time it is?

Lee was about to say something but Jared cut him off.

Ramshaw will eat us alive if we're late.

Jared opened the bathroom door and kept it open. Lee swore as he let go of my arm.

Have a good day, mutant, Owen whispered as he followed Lee into the hallway.

But it wasn't my day I was thinking about as I watched the three of them walk toward the gym. It was what they were going to tell Ryan.

Ryan knows a lot of things.

He gets 90s in science. He aces math. When he was ten he cooked up a science fair project that was mentioned in a medical magazine. He wrote an essay in the sixth grade that Ms. Haverstock laminated so she could pass it around for the next fifty years.

He's an honor roll student, and if there was a dishonor roll, he would be on that too. Ryan knows a heck of a lot.

But he doesn't know about my binder.

Mr. Lam looked at me like me like I was holding a grenade and not a small box.

You drink tea?

Yes, I lied. I didn't feel like explaining. The tea was for Sean. He had texted me that morning to say he wasn't feeling well and was staying home. He asked me to stop by McCreary's Good-Luck-Finding-It-on-the-Corner Store after school, since his mother wanted him to drink buckets of green tea.

Mr. Lam kept staring at the box in my hand. I could tell he didn't believe me. The only drinks kids ever buy in his store come out of cans.

Green tea is good for cancer, he said.

I know.

Mr. Lam tapped his chest. **It makes the heart very, very strong.**

You bet, I said. **My grandmother drank it until she was a hundred and seven.**

Lies are like potato chips. It's hard to stop at just one. And part of me wanted Mr. Lam to like me. More like, fewer grunts. I thought I saw a quick, stiff smile when he handed me my change. It might have been a wince.

When I stepped outside, Ruby was sitting in the same spot she had been sitting in when I had gone into her father's store. It didn't look like she had moved an inch. She was holding a piece of chalk in her hand and staring at the bland-as-porridge sidewalk.

I had to double-check to make sure it was blank.

Can I ask you a question?

Ruby nodded.

What are you doing?

Ruby didn't answer at first. No one expects you to say a heck of a lot when you speak Shy. I was about to walk away when she said, **Drawing**.

Drawing?

Ruby placed a finger on her head. **First I draw in here.** She pointed to the drab sidewalk. **Then I make an outside drawing.**

You draw the whole picture in your head first?

She nodded.

You see it before it's there.

A small Ruby nod and a small Ruby smile. That was why it was such a short way between *decide* and *done* when she made a drawing. Half the work was complete before she even started.

And after you're finished, your mother washes it away. I had seen Ruby's mother scrub the sidewalk. **Like the next day or something.**

Ruby nodded. **Then I start again,** she said.

I had a feeling it was Mr. Lam who sent Mrs. Lam outside with a bucket and brush. If it was up to Mrs. Lam, the block would be corner-to-corner Ruby. I looked at the sidewalk that wouldn't be drab for long.

Can I take a picture? Before you start drawing?

Ruby nodded. I took a photograph of the boring, blank sidewalk and her tin of chalk. It's called *Possibilities.*

You can't see the possibilities unless you're a Ruby.

I thought of the sidewalk where Lucy always used to sit. People walked around her the same way they walked around Ruby's drawings. It looked like the same walk but the walks said different things. One said Step Around. The other said Step Away.

I started toward Sean's house. Then I turned back. Ruby had begun to draw.

If you want, I can take pictures of some of your drawings. Before your mother scrubs them off.

Ruby said, **Yes, please.**

Her voice was as soft as chalk on sidewalk.

That's another reason why we need photographs. To remember what was there before it disappears.

It took three knocks before Sean's apartment door finally opened.

He looked pale and hadn't brushed his hair. His shirt wasn't buttoned properly. He had a bandage on one hand.

I got your green tea.

Sean said **Thanks** and looked like he was about to say something else when Watson showed up and started nibbling on my shoe. Sean grabbed his collar and pulled him back.

You don't want him to get too close.

I looked at Watson. He seemed as surprised as I felt. **Why not?** I asked.

Sean turned around and walked into his living room. Watson followed him every step of the way. I closed the door behind me. I had a feeling Watson knew he was in trouble and thought that the closer he stuck to Sean the less trouble he would be in. Sean waited for me to sit down on the couch. He kept standing.

Watson bit me.

Watson? I said. All Watson ever did was lick people. In the world according to Watson, everyone was an ice-cream cone. Every face was his favorite flavor.

Sean lifted up his shirt. There was a long piece of gauze taped to one side of his stomach. Then he held up his bandaged hand.

Watson?

He nodded. He tucked his shirt in and sat down. He said they'd been wrestling on his bed like they'd done a thousand times before, only this time Watson **went over the edge.**

I looked at Watson. He spent so much time getting into trouble that he never had enough time to get out of it. But the trouble he got into was normal trouble. It was eat-the-gluten-free-cake-Sean's-mother-spent-all-morning-baking trouble. It was grab-and-bury-an-electrician's-screwdriver trouble. It was break-Sean's-globe-and-swallow-Australia trouble. It was never gauze-on-cut trouble.

I asked him what green tea did for cuts.

Sean shrugged. **My mother wants me to drink it. And she says Watson has to go to obedience school.**

Doesn't he deserve a second chance?

He shook his head. He looked even paler. **A second chance could mean a third bite. My mother says this has to be nipped in the bud.** He stood up. **Our first class is this afternoon.**

I thought you had to stay home.

He lifted Watson's leash off its hook. **Mom thought I could use some fresh air.**

Want me to go with you?

Sean shook his head and rubbed Watson's head at the same time. **Not this time,** he said. **But there's something you have to do really soon, T—. For us.**

I wasn't sure who the "us" was. Sean and Watson? Sean and me? Me, Sean, and Watson? I just said, **What do you want me to do?**

Show the photographs to Ms. Karamath. Please. He clipped the leash to Watson's collar. **Why are you waiting?**

Sean didn't hang around for me to answer. He walked me to the door with Watson by his side. He looked at Watson as if everything he loved about him had gone away and all that was left was Watson-on-the-outside. Inside was a different dog. A Watson that bit and scratched Sean.

I hope the old Watson comes back soon, I said.

Sean didn't say anything when we stepped out of his apartment building and headed in different directions. No **See ya**. No **Later**. He kept his head down and kept looking at Watson. It was like the Sean I knew had left for good and all that was left was Sean-on-the-outside.

The outside-only Sean and Watson made me want to spend time inside the Vault. Everything there was familiar. Everything was always in its place.

After I got to the Goodison Building I climbed up the stairs two by two to the second floor. I was about to open the door when I stopped.

The door wasn't closed. There was a photograph of an old woman on the floor in the gap between where the door was and where it should have been. The photograph had been ripped in two so all I saw was the woman's eyes and her ripped and wrinkled cheeks.

I slowly opened the door. What I saw made me feel like my insides had been scooped out.

Nearly all the photographs had been torn off the walls, which suddenly looked naked. Some were torn in half. Others were torn to shreds. The too-broken-to-fix lamp had been knocked down and bent out of shape. The bread box lid was ripped clean off its hinges. The box was smashed into too many pieces to count. The shattered alarm clock was all crack and no clock.

There were handfuls of old, once-was-yellow foam all over the floor. Ryan had torn the truck seat apart. I wondered for a moment if he had been looking for *Lucy's Last Moments*. He must have figured I didn't end up on the second floor of an abandoned building unless I wanted to be there. And I would probably only want to be there if there was something there waiting for me.

The Vault had always been a spot no one would find on a map no one had. Now I felt as if a gleeful Ryan had found the map and was grinding it into my face.

I sat on the passenger side of what was left of the truck seat and looked at the mess Hurricane Ryan had left behind. I thought of the photographs I had seen of people who had survived natural disasters. Earthquakes and monsoons and tsunamis. They all look the same, dazed and dented and out of batteries.

As I slowly picked up the unripped photos and carefully put them back on the walls, I wondered what was next. Would Ryan attack me? Steal my camera and send it back in pieces? It's not like I could knock on his door and find out. I needed someone's help to prevent the next next, and I knew who to ask.

I stared at the gnomes.

There were three of them planted in Jared's front yard. They all had the same pointy hat, the same white beard, the same permanent smile (one did a lousy job of covering his up). They were Ryan smiles. You couldn't tell what was behind them.

The truth was, I didn't know Jared. I didn't know if he would slam the door in my face or make a threat that would eat at me until there wasn't much of me left. I didn't know if he would pretend to ignore me but actually listen or pretend to listen but actually ignore me. For all I knew, there were ten different Jareds, and I didn't know which one would show up at the door.

I didn't tell Sean I planned to speak to Jared. I had decided he was the best chance I had to get Ryan to lay off. I knew it was a long shot but I figured if a blank sidewalk had possibilities, maybe Just Jared did too. Maybe the flicker I had seen in the bathroom when he stopped Owen and Lee from doing any real damage to me was the flicker I needed to stop Ryan.

After about ten deep breaths I walked up and knocked on the front door. A minute later it swung open. I knew the woman standing there had to be Jared's mother because they looked identical, even though I had never seen Jared in a red dress or wearing a headband and hoop earrings. Her smile was so warm and genuine a gnome would be envious.

Are you here for Jared?

I nodded. She stepped back into the house.

Jared, she yelled. **A friend's here to see you.**

I'm not a friend, I unsaid.

A minute later Jared was at the door. When he saw me, he tried to act like he wasn't surprised. His mother disappeared inside.

What do you want?

I had rehearsed what I was going to say to Jared a thousand times, but all the words took off like startled birds until I was left with only five.

You know what really happened.

It didn't look like I needed to say any more. Jared looked back in the house, then he stepped closer, pulling the door behind him. It wasn't quite shut but he was outside.

What are you talking about?

Jared's words and face were on two different channels. He sounded annoyed but he looked concerned.

What you did to Lucy.

When he said **Who?** it sounded so hollow I'm surprised it didn't float away like one of Bubbles Bianco's bubbles.

I took a photograph from my back pocket that I had grabbed as I left the Vault. It was one of the few that Ryan hadn't torn off the walls or ripped into pieces.

That's who.

Before I knew it Jared had the photograph in his own hand and was staring at it. I figured he was going to glance at it for a second and then pretend he was Ryan and toss it. I didn't expect him to take it. I don't think he did either.

In the photograph Lucy is looking up at something, only you can't see what that "something" is. Maybe it's a plane. Maybe it's a bird. Maybe it's a balloon. That's why *Swing* is one of my favorite Lucy pictures. It's about what you can't see.

Know what I think?

Jared looked up. He was pale.

I think you know it was wrong.

I tried reading his face but it was totally blank.

You should tell the truth. I bet your mother would help you. It wasn't what I planned to say but it felt right. She looked like she had lots of flicker to go around. **Go to the police and tell them what happened to Lucy. You're not like Ryan and Med. You know you're not like them. They're gutless. You've got something in you they don't.** I couldn't tell how much of what I said was sticking to Jared. **Man up**, I said. That's what Mr. Ramshaw says to kickstart kids running low on flow.

Who's that?

Jared's sister, Olive, had stepped out of the house. She was pointing to the picture of Lucy.

She looks nice, she said.

Jared swung the door open. **Get inside!** He pushed Olive in and shut the door behind her.

Olive had brought him back from wherever *Swing* had taken him. He turned around and called me only one name, but sometimes the sting of one word can do the work of twenty.

You know it was wrong, I said again. **And I think it's eating you up.**

Neither of us said a word. We both stared at *Swing*.

Are you boys going to stand there all day? Jared's mother called from inside the house. **There's nachos and cheese in the oven.**

Jared took a long, deep breath. For a few seconds I thought he might step into the kitchen and tell his mother the truth.

T— has a soccer game, Jared said. **He came by to borrow a book.**

Some lies come with accessories. Jared went into his house, and when he returned a minute later, he didn't have *Swing* with him. He was holding a copy of *Animal Farm* instead. He handed me the book and said, **No one tells me what to do.**

Except Ryan, I said.

Jared laughed a scripted laugh. He made a point of saying, **Have a good game**, loudly before he closed the door.

I walked away, then turned back. I thought I saw Jared watching me through the living room curtains. Whoever was there wasn't there for long.

I looked at the gnomes. They were smiling their identical smiles and wearing their identical hats. They would never change.

One more.

Ms. Karamath laid a photograph on the table in front of me.

His name is Tank Man.

If you're going to call yourself Tank Man, you better look special. You don't have to wear superhero tights or some getup that catches everyone's attention and doesn't let go. But you better not call yourself Tank Man and then just look like you're heading home with a shopping bag in each hand, which is what this guy was holding.

Only he's facing a long row of tanks.

If it was just a picture of a row of tanks, you wouldn't look twice. But Tank Man stands right in front of the first tank like he's daring it to roll forward. Like he's forgotten he's only holding shopping bags in each hand and not sticks of tank-twisting dynamite. Like he doesn't realize he's ten seconds away from becoming tank food. When most people see a tank rolling toward them, they run the other way. Tank Man wasn't most people.

Ms. Karamath told me that in 1989, after days of protests against the Communist government in China, tanks rolled into Tiananmen Square in Beijing **to crush dissent**. One look at those tanks and you know it's not just dissent that gets crushed. The protest must have been shaken out of every protestor because the street is empty. Except for Tank Man.

Ms. Karamath explained that he was called Tank Man because

no one knew his real name. **He took a stand**, she said. **He's the picture of courage.**

I nodded. I stared at the photograph. Anyone who likes the photograph couldn't like Tank Man's odds. He was David versus Goliath but at least David had a stone. How far can you get smacking a tank with a shopping bag?

The confrontation didn't last long, said Ms. Karamath. Eventually Tank Man was moved away, though **it's up in the air** as to who did the moving. **There's doubt about his fate** — he was executed, he went into hiding, he's still alive — **but there's no denying a singular moment has endured.**

Some people drop names. Ms. Karamath drops words. After "singular" landed in my lap, I knew she would expect me to take it apart.

I'll leave you to immerse yourself in the photograph.

I immersed myself. I stared at the man staring down the tank. I stared for a long time.

And then it happened. It doesn't happen very often, but when it does you remember it forever. You become a photograph.

I was Tank Man. Ryan was the tank.

I knew it would take more than shopping bags to stop him. I knew I would need help and it would be hard to be heard. There weren't a lot of doors I wanted to knock on.

Except one.

Ms. Karamath's office is the exact opposite of Bubbles Bianco's office, which is so messy it needs to be mowed. Everything in Ms. Karamath's office is neat and organized into binders. Every binder has a label and is arranged alphabetically on shelves. A *B* binder wouldn't have time to say hello to a *P* binder before it was yanked away and put where it belongs.

I knocked on the office door. Ms. Karamath was at her desk. She looked up and invited me in.

I stepped forward. **Can only adults take a photograph that makes a difference?**

She smiled. **Art is not like driving a car or casting a vote, T—. It can be made by anyone, anytime and anywhere. There are no age restrictions.**

She asked me why I wanted to know.

I took a deep breath. It was so deep I felt my head spin. Ms. Karamath asked me if I was okay. I didn't answer. I just said it.

I have a photograph that can make a difference.

I touched the dog tag under my shirt.

A bunch of photographs.

Ms. Karamath smiled again. It was a real smile. A 100-percent smile. No artificial ingredients.

I'd like to see them.

I nodded.

Then my cell phone went off.

Ms. Karamath's smile disappeared. Her lips twist-tied. She's hyper-strict about cell phones ringing in the library. Usually she takes them away and doesn't give them back until you've written a five-hundred-word essay about Cell Phone Etiquette.

All she said was **Turn it off.**

I took the phone out of my pocket. It was a text from Sean.

Watson is dead.

I called Sean as soon as I stepped out of the library and out the front doors. I was surprised when his mother answered his phone. She said Sean had found Watson lying on his bed, stretched out across the pillows (his favorite spot), looking less and less like Watson until there was no Watson left. They didn't know what had happened. There was no time to get to the vet. There was no point. Watson died with Sean's arms around him. She said Sean needed some alone time with Watson and suggested I come the next day.

When I got there on Saturday morning Sean's mother answered the door. Sean hadn't come out of his room since the night before. She said Marek, the superintendent, had given them permission to bury Watson in the backyard. The funeral would be that day.

Sean stepped into the living room, looking as shattered as a flower vase Watson had once knocked over. Sean's mother glued it back together, but the vase was never the same (it leaked). I wondered if Sean ever would be either.

Before you say your final good-byes, you might want to spend some time in the park, Sean's mother said. **I can't think of a place with more memories of Watson.**

Sean carried Watson's leash as we walked over. It was hard watching him hold it without Watson at the other end.

We have more memories than there is park, I said. **And it's a big park.** I didn't expect Sean to say much, so I was pleased to get a quiet **Yup.**

About ten minutes after we arrived, a sheep dog ran up to Sean and knocked him over.

No, Alfie! a woman wearing a baseball cap yelled.

Alfie must have thought Sean was a new snack because he kept licking him and only stopped when his owner pulled him off.

I'm sorry, she said. **This dog is incorrigible!**

Sean said he didn't mind.

After Alfie was dragged away, Sean and I went to the playground where many little kids had been Watsonned. Ice-cream cones had been snatched out of little hands (and replaced with new ones, which made Watson both incorrigible and expensive). Plastic buckets were nabbed out of sandboxes. Once, he grabbed a loose sandal hanging from the foot of a young girl swinging on a swing. He ran in two-way circles with the sandal, changing directions each time Sean caught up with him. The little girl laughed one of those little-kid laughs that go on for so long you wonder if the kid's battery is going to last. When Sean returned the sandal, he was expecting an icy stare. He got a warm smile instead, and the girl's mother thanked him for a story she would share for years.

We were sitting by the monkey bars. Sean had curled the leash into a small loop. I reminded him about the sandal story. **Watson's not here**, I said, **but Watson stories can last for a really long time**.

He laughed and squeezed the leash. **He gave us more stories than trouble.**

We spent half an hour sharing Watson stories. We could have spent another week but I knew we couldn't wait that long. We had to head back to Sean's place and do what Sean didn't want to do. I didn't want to do it either.

If there's something you really don't want to do, it helps to have someone help you not do it.

Not right away.

Not for a while.

Not until you're ready.

I don't know what to say.

Sean looked at the hole he had dug for Watson.

I told him he didn't have to say anything. I was sure there was a written-out ceremony online for burying dead pets, but it was probably full of mushy things and Sean wasn't interested in mush.

Sean carefully picked up the shroud that Watson was wrapped in. He didn't want to bury him without anything to cover and protect him, so his mother cut up Sean's pillowcases and sewed them together. It looked beautiful, with a green vine along the edges and Watson's name in red thread.

You were a good dog, Sean told the pillowcase.

He looked at me and asked if I had anything to tell Watson. I had never spoken to a dead dog before, and I hadn't spent a heck of a lot of time talking to Watson when he was alive. But I could tell Sean wanted me to say something. When you've been in the same boat with someone for a long time, you learn to speak Boat.

Thanks, Watson.

I couldn't think of anything else to say. Then I added, **If there's a dog heaven, don't cause too much trouble.**

Sean smiled a quarter-smile. It was probably the biggest smile he could come up with.

He placed Watson in the hole. We both stood by it. Sean put his hand on the handle of the shovel, which was wedged in a mound of dirt.

He didn't move. He was so still it looked like everything was attached. Mound-shovel-Sean. Mound-shovel-Sean.

I can't do it.

He stepped away, so now it was just mound-shovel.

I can't do it, he said again.

I didn't say anything because I could tell he wanted to say something else.

I can't throw dirt onto Watson. He looked down at the bag in the hole. **I can't do it.**

If it was a Diane Arbus photograph, it would have been called *Boy Standing Next to Shovel and Hole in Ground.* You would wonder what was in the hole and why he was looking at it. You wouldn't know about the boy outside the photograph, who took the shovel out of the mound and started shoveling dirt into the hole while the other boy watched. Neither one said a word.

When the boy-outside-the-picture finished moving all the dirt back where it belonged, the other boy nodded. They both looked at where the hole had been. Then the boy-outside-the-picture walked away so the other boy could be alone with the filled hole.

I went up the back stairs to Sean's third-floor apartment. I sat down at the kitchen table and his mother gave me a molasses cookie shaped like a bone. **A small tribute to a dog with a big heart**, she said.

I nibbled on the cookie, expecting it to taste like sawdust. It was sweet and chewy. I grabbed another one, not knowing if Sean's mother would ever get it right again.

She touched my head, quickly but gently. **Where were you when I was Sean's age and heartbroken?**

I smiled but couldn't get further than a half smile. It was impossible to picture Sean's mother at thirteen. I knew my parents were once kids too. But in all the photos of them before I was born, they look like they're auditioning to be my parents and are too young to get the parts.

When Sean stepped into the kitchen, his mother held up a molasses bone.

I'm not hungry.

Sean's mother stood up and gave him a bear hug.

I didn't think you would be, sweetheart. Maybe later.

Maybe.

We went back to Sean's room but we weren't there for five minutes before he said, **You want to take a walk?**

I nodded. We were about a block away from Sean's apartment when he suddenly stopped. I went a few more steps before I realized he wasn't beside me. I turned around. He stood as statue-still as he had been next to Watson's grave. He looked both ways. He looked across the street. Then he pulled something out of his back pocket and handed it to me.

It was an envelope with his name on it. I opened it.

With Deepest Sympathy the card said on the cover.

Inside: *May you find comfort in the love of family, in the warmth of friends.*

The word "friends" had been crossed out. Someone had written "Scarface" in red pen. That was what Joined at the Hip called me on better days.

I looked at the card and wondered if Ryan had an ounce of sympathy in him. If he did, it would have been a very lonely ounce.

There's one more thing, Sean said. **On the back.**

I turned the card over and saw four red-pen words. *Man Up. Dog Down.*

I felt something inside me split open. My talk with Jared backfired big time. I had been hoping Jared would talk to someone and put Ryan where he belonged. I never expected a dead dog wrapped in a pillowcase.

I don't even know what that means, Sean said. **Do you?**

I shrugged.

The card was waiting for me after school. Watson was still alive. Barely.

I had never heard Sean not-cry before. He shoved his fists into his cheeks like he was trying to stuff his tears back inside. It wasn't working.

They poisoned him, T—.

I felt like my body was on fire. I wanted to throttle Ryan with hands made of flames.

Sean continued to walk and didn't stop until we reached a drive-way between two apartment buildings. He pointed to a garage door covered with graffiti. **That's where they cornered me. They said they'd seen you one morning, talking to Bianco.**

Early birds thinking they had caught me in the act.

They told me if you said anything, they'd cut off part of my tongue. They wanted me to make sure you knew that.

I told Sean I hadn't said a word to Bubbles Bianco.

I said you had a mind of your own.

I tried to picture what happened next. **Then what?**

Sean lifted his shirt and showed me where Watson had taken a bite out of him. It was still red and sore.

This wasn't Watson.

He tucked his shirt in and lifted his bandaged hand.

This wasn't Watson either.

I looked at Sean. He had that look when you scrub a lie off your face so the truth can come through.

Watson never needed obedience lessons, I said.

Sean shook his head. **I blamed Watson so my mother wouldn't know what had really happened.**

He looked at me. Some people look at my scars and don't bother seeing much else. It's like the scars are the Eiffel Tower and the rest of me is France. Sean knows there's a heck of a lot more to France than the Eiffel Tower.

Did you show Ms. Karamath *Lucy's Last Moments*? he asked.

I'll show her tomorrow morning, I said. **First thing.**

Don't.

Sometimes, a single word can knock you down faster than a whole herd.

Why not?

Sean stepped aside and waited for a woman pushing a stroller to pass us before he continued.

It starts with a dog. You think that's where it stops? Ryan killed Watson.

I nodded.

It might not stop there.

I nodded again.

Evil is a lightless path.

A line from one of Sean's mystery novels.

Go to Ms. Karamath and Ryan will drag you down that path.

I shook my head. **Let's keep walking.**

We walked for about a block and reached a row of small houses. I looked around. There was a birdbath on one lawn and a tricycle on another.

It took me a few seconds to realize what Sean was doing because what he was doing wasn't something Sean would normally ever do. He was trying to tear the dog tag off my neck.

I grabbed his hand. **Let go!**

We both said it at the same time.

The chain was digging into my neck as Sean pulled at the tag. I dug my fingers deep into the hand Sean had around the tag. I don't know how much digging and dugging we did before we both ended up on the ground, rolling around on a lawn.

Cut that out!

A woman walked toward us. She was wearing gardening gloves and holding a trowel. She had angry eyes and dirt on her knees.

You are going to crush my perennials. Just crush them. She jabbed the air with the trowel. **Take your wrestling match somewhere else.**

Sean and I didn't move. He hadn't let go of the memory stick. I hadn't let go of his hand. We were both trying to catch our breath. It wasn't close to getting caught.

Did you not hear me the first time?

She sprayed us with a hose. Sean let go of the memory stick, which I covered with my hand to keep dry.

Now do I have your attention?

She did. She turned off the hose but held the nozzle like a gun. We didn't want to mess with an armed gardener. Sean and I picked ourselves up, brushing the grass off as we walked away.

Neither of us said anything for about five minutes.

When we came to a bus stop, Sean suddenly stopped and sat down. **I'm sorry**, he said.

Same here.

Sean looked straight ahead when he spoke.

I don't want you to get hurt.

I know.

He turned to face me. The look on his face wasn't a look I had ever seen for as long as I had known him. He was so filled with fear there wasn't room for a drop of anything else.

You don't know. This isn't like before.

Sean leaned forward, searching for the bus we wouldn't take. We were only five blocks from his apartment.

Lucy's dead, he said. **Watson's dead. You could be next.**

Sean put his hand on my knee and left it there. The bus arrived a minute later. He pulled his hand away when the bus doors opened. We didn't move.

You don't need a bus, I said, **when you have a boat.**

The bus driver shook his head, shut the doors, and drove off.

I don't know how long we sat there before we stood up and rowed home.

Binders aren't like books. You can unbind a binder. You can't unbook a book.

A book full of lies is always a book full of lies. There's no way to add the truth.

A bindered story is different. If Ryan knew about Binder No. 1, he would shred all the truths in it and then burn the shreds. But with a binder, you can always put the truth back in if it goes missing. Or if it shows up later.

Some days I think I ended up where I am because of a cement truck.

I went to school early on Monday morning to show Ms. Karamath *Lucy's Last Moments*. I didn't care what Sean said or what Joined at the Hip might do to me. I wanted to break my silence and needed her help breaking it. Sometimes a photograph can make a difference. I thought Ms. Karamath could make a difference too.

Only Ms. Karamath wasn't there. When I stepped into the library, a woman with big purple glasses and chunky purple earrings smiled at me. She was short but wore a long skirt and a lot of bracelets that jingled when she walked. She told me her name was Mrs. Cappel and that Ms. Karamath had been in **a car accident** but that it wasn't serious and that they expected she would be back **soon**.

How soon? I unasked.

Is there something I can help you with?

I said, **No, thank you**.

Mrs. Cappel smiled and jingled away.

I grabbed a book off a shelf, sat down, and pretended to read. Everything I wanted to tell Ms. Karamath was still bottled up inside of me.

It's nice to see a boy take such an active interest in sewing.

Mrs. Cappel tapped a nail-polished finger (purple) on an illustration in the book I had been pretending to read. It was of a girl wearing a green dress. I turned the page. There was a picture of the same dress, without the girl. Beneath the dress were a bunch of instructions.

I had paid zero attention to what was inside the book I had grabbed off the shelf. It was called *Making the Cut: Sewing for the Modern Teen*. I could tell Mrs. Cappel was the kind of teacher who couldn't wait to help me choose the right buttons. (Right = purple.)

I closed the book. **Do you think Ms. Karamath will be back this week?**

She shrugged and smiled and jingled. As she walked away I noticed Owen and Joined at the Hip at a nearby table. They stood up and walked toward me.

You got something to show Ms. K.? Med asked.

Something to tell her? Jared added.

Show-and-tell is for little kids, Owen said. He picked up the book. **Not for modern teens.**

They all looked at stone-faced Ryan, who was staring at me, not saying a word. I was waiting for him to speak. I wanted him to speak. Otherwise I had to fill in the blanks. One of the worst sounds in the world is a blank waiting to be filled.

After a week of blankness Ryan turned and walked out of the library. His sheep followed.

When I woke up the next morning I thought I was dreaming.

An awake dream is worse than an asleep dream. A bad asleep dream is unplugged the second you wake up. But bad awake dreams don't come with plugs or batteries or a switch. You can rub your eyes all you want but it will still be there. "It" is what made you rub your eyes in the first place.

It was a photograph. *Boy with Dog.* But Watson was cut out of the photograph while Sean had a thick red *X* over his face. It covered his eyes, nose, and mouth.

It wasn't there when I had gone to sleep.

I don't know how long I sat on my bed without moving. My mother knocked on my door and said, **Are you awake?**

I didn't answer.

She knocked two more times and was about to open my bedroom door when I yelled, **I'm getting dressed**.

My mother said, **Someone woke up on the wrong side of the bed**, and walked away.

I wished I had woken up on the right side of the bed. All I could see from the wrong side was *Boy Without Dog*. And the Boy's smile was smothered by an X. Ryan must have stolen the photo when he ransacked the Vault.

I pictured him in my bedroom, placing the photograph on the dresser, standing by my bed, smirking as I slept. He had filled in the blank. I felt sick.

I put what was left of *Boy with Dog* in my drawer. (It's still there.)

That's when I noticed my laptop was open. I had closed it the night before.

Ryan must have searched it for the Lucy photographs. When he didn't find them, he broke letters off the keyboard and arranged them in a row.

WATCH YOURSELF.

When I got to school, Sean wasn't there.

I texted him but he didn't text back.

I saw Ryan standing by his locker, showing Jared and Med something on his cell phone. They were laughing. I wondered if he was showing them pictures of my bedroom. A picture of me, asleep.

Then I realized: For all I knew, Ryan went from my house to Sean's house in the middle of the night and *X*d Sean. And not with a red marker.

I texted Sean five times before the bell rang but he didn't text back. I waited for the right time during class. Ms. Garvey was teaching us about some Russian dog that had been sent into orbit. I thought of Watson and all the trouble he had caused down on Earth. He would have chewed on anything he found in space. We'd never have a full moon again.

I worried how long I'd have a Sean.

I texted him again. Still no reply.

Ten texts later I still hadn't heard from Sean. I wasn't going to wait seven weeks for the lunch bell to ring. I asked Ms. Garvey if I could go the bathroom. When I stepped out of the classroom I hesitated for a split second, but the split wasn't big enough to change my mind. I knew I'd get a bubble-filled lecture about truancy but I didn't care. I ran down a hallway and out a back door. I didn't stop running until I got to Sean's building.

I expected to see yellow police tape around it and an ambulance in front. All I saw was Marek, the superintendent, singing a song about a place called Heartbreak Hotel as he fixed a lawn mower.

When I knocked on Sean's door no one answered. My heart was halfway up my throat.

Two knocks later I heard him say, **Hang on.**

I was so relieved to hear his voice. I didn't know I had that much relief in me.

When he opened the door, he looked surprised to see me. Usually I get a *Hey* or a *Hi*. He just stood in the doorway, looking pale.

Are you okay? I asked.

I waited for Sean to answer or to let me in. He didn't do either.

What are you doing here?

I wanted to see if you were all right. Sean looked like he wasn't anywhere near All Right and would need a lift to get there. **Are you?**

I guess.

He didn't sound convinced or convincing.

Can I come in?

Sean stepped back. I followed him into his kitchen. I was surprised to see the counter was full of normal fruit. Sean's mother usually buys fruit you've never seen from countries you've never heard of and makes foreign-country fruit salads. Sean was cutting up apples, kiwis, and bananas.

My mom has a massive migraine.

When Sean's mother has a migraine, she lies in bed and can't move. Sean stays home to make sure she has what she needs.

I asked him if he needed any help. He said, **No thanks.**

I wasn't sure what to do, so I sat down at the kitchen table.

Halfway through a banana Sean turned to me and said he was sorry.

For what?

He sliced the rest of the banana before he said anything.

Ryan was here last night.

In your apartment?

He shook his head. He had started to cut an apple.

We met downstairs. He wanted your locker combination.

He took a deep breath.

I thought of Watson and how they —

Sean stopped talking and kept slicing. He was crying these silent tears. Some landed on the apple.

I'm sorry, he said to a grapefruit. Sometimes it's easier to face a grapefruit than a friend. **I was up all night.**

I bet Ryan was too, I unsaid.

I don't care if they get into my locker, I said. There was nothing inside that was worth stealing. **They'll mark up my photographs and think it's really funny.**

Sean nodded slowly. He arranged all the fruit on a plate and then carried the plate into his mother's bedroom.

Only when I was alone in the kitchen did I notice it.

I couldn't stand standing there by myself, so I stepped softly toward Sean's mother's bedroom to say a quick good-bye.

Sean's mother was lying on her bed, covered in a blanket, as still as stone. She had a cloth over her forehead and eyes. Sean took a half slice of apple and gently placed it in her mouth like she was a baby bird. He handled a kiwi slice like it was this rare coin. I don't know what Sean's mother would have done without him, and I didn't want to find out.

I didn't say good-bye. I didn't want to bother his mom. I just left the apartment and waved to Marek on my way out of the building. He smiled a big smile and I smiled a big smile, but my smile collapsed a second later. All I could think of was Sean, Lucy, and Ryan, and none of them were smiling.

The truth is as easy to crop as a photograph.

Ryan called me on my cell phone. He didn't bother with **Hello** or even **Is this the dipstick?** He just said, **You have ten minutes to get to Thank God It's Sundae**. Then he hung up.

It was a Tuesday night. My father was streaming something pre-historic called *I Dream of Jeannie* (and I have a feeling he dreamed of her until at least Friday). I told my mother I was going out to get ice cream, which was true but it wasn't the whole truth. It was a cropped truth.

Ten minutes later I saw Ryan sitting on a bench, eating a sundae. He was all smiles when he saw me. When I sat down beside him, he handed me a sundae of my own.

I hope you like hot fudge. You look like a hot-fudge man. Am I right?

I shook my head. **Strawberry.**

I could see Ryan was annoyed for a split second. He hates being wrong, even when it comes to me and sundaes.

Pretend the hot fudge is strawberry.

I wasn't going to pretend I was eating something I wasn't, but I wasn't going to argue with Ryan either.

Every spoonful was a hot fudge spoonful. I wondered how many spoonfuls it would take before Ryan would tell me what he wanted. After seven quick spoonfuls, he still hadn't spoken. By spoonful ten, I decided to say something.

I'm not afraid of you.

I don't know why I said it. I wasn't sure I even meant it. I think what I meant was I wasn't afraid of being afraid.

Afraid? Ryan sucked on his spoon like it was a lollipop. **Why would you be afraid of me?**

You broke into my house, I unsaid. *You poisoned Sean's dog. You've threatened to kill my best friend.*

What do you want?

He tapped on my sundae cup. **I want you to slow down. Enjoy your strawberry sundae. We've got time to kill.**

I looked at Ryan. He had killed more than just time.

Every few minutes he got a text. He read each message and smiled. After I had finished my sundae, I stood up to toss the cup in the trash. Ryan pulled me back down.

Not yet, Romeo.

I tried to pretend I wasn't rattled. Joined at the Hip had never been around to hear Lucy call me Romeo. She must have mentioned me during her last moments. I felt sick.

Sundae didn't agree with you?

I stood up again. **I'm leaving.**

Ryan grabbed me. **Not yet.**

Yes, yet, I said.

Where're your manners, Romeo? I buy you an ice cream and you take off?

I looked into Ryan's eyes. There was no life there.

I have things to do.

Ryan kept his hand on my wrist and pulled me down toward the bench. **So do I.**

But then we just sat there. After about five more minutes and three more texts, he let go of my wrist and said, **Let's do it again sometime.**

He grinned a Ryan grin and slapped me on my back.

I stood up and walked away. I didn't look back. I waited until I was around the corner, and then I ran home.

35

You were gone a long time.

I had just stepped through the front door. I told my mother, **I lost track of time.**

You can be like that sometimes. How long does it take to get ice cream?

She walked away and didn't wait for an answer because it wasn't that kind of question. It's the kind of question you ask when you want to make a point. Maybe that's why question marks look like hooks. *All the better to snag you with, my dear.*

I was in my room when I heard a flock of sirens wailing outside. If it's only one siren, then I know it's a police car or maybe just one fire truck. If it's only one fire truck, then it's just a false alarm or a small fire like a burning trash can. But a flock of sirens means a big fire that registers at least a 250 on the Zito scale.

I grabbed my jacket and ran downstairs. My parents are used to seeing me rush toward the door when they hear sirens. **Where's the fire?** my father always says, which is his idea of a joke. My mother adds, **Keep a safe distance**, and I say, **Promise**, which is a half lie because my definition of "safe" and my mother's definition aren't in the same dictionary.

I stepped outside and saw some smoke a few blocks over. Another fire truck came wailing down the street and turned about three blocks away. It was a warm night, which means there was going to be a lot more moths than if there was snow on the ground. I prefer watching fires in the winter because there's hardly anyone around.

I reached the corner where I saw the fire truck make a left turn. I'd been down this street about a million times. Maybe one of the stores I knew was up in smoke. Some store owners speak Ignore but a few are nice enough. One guy owns a flower store and sometimes he gives me half-dead flowers that he doesn't think anyone will buy. *Give them to your wife*, he always says, and I smile and pretend I haven't heard the joke before. I give the flowers to my mother and she never seems to mind that they're half-dead. Some people are glass-half-empty people. My mother is flowers-half-alive.

I passed the flower store and started to run because some other moths were running. My heart was pounding before I turned the corner. The fire trucks were still two blocks from me but I could see the flames. I could smell the smoke.

The Vault was on fire.

Running those last two blocks was like running through water.

By the time I joined the other moths in front of the building, it was an 850 on the Zito scale and climbing. The front part of the building was a wall of fire.

I couldn't move. I could feel the heat but I was frozen stiff.

At least it was empty.

A thin man with stringy hair was trying to make small talk with me. He looked like a scarecrow. His arms were too long for his jacket. His pants were too short for his legs.

They got all those homeless people out.

I didn't want to make small talk, big talk, or any kind of talk. I said, **Yeah**, and then I turned and looked at the flames. They looked like they were dancing.

I didn't tell the scarecrow that empty buildings can keep secrets. I was glad the homeless people escaped but my collection of photographs was still inside. I had remounted or replaced just about all my photos after Hurricane Ryan. Laughing people, pouting people, before-and-after people. Every picture brings something to life, and every life in the Vault had been smothered by thick black smoke. There was something ironic about burn-victim photographs turning to ash, I thought. A collection that had taken years to put together was destroyed in minutes.

Something inside me felt like the kid in *Child with Toy Hand Grenade in Central Park, NYC*. I wasn't holding a toy grenade and I wasn't in Central Park but I thought I would explode.

A firefighter was climbing up a truck with a rear-mount ladder. When he reached the top, he aimed the hose at the building the same easy way people water their front lawns. He was totally in control. He was as cool as a cucumber.

Enjoying yourself, mutant?

Ryan stood right next to me, chewing on his sundae spoon. I looked around. He was sheepless. I saw Scarecrow taking pictures of the fire with his cell phone and thought Ryan was like the Tin Man. Hollow inside. No heart. Never without his ax.

I'm not a mutant, I said.

He smiled.

You know what you really are? He looked at me as if I was way more interesting than flames and hoses. **You're in trouble.**

Ryan walked away. Scarecrow came up to me again, still holding his cell phone. He wanted me to get a picture of him with the fire behind him, like we were at Niagara Falls or on top of the Empire State Building. He smiled, the building roared, and I took a picture. Scarecrow thanked me and told me to have a good evening.

There was this loud groan and some moths started to scream.

The roof! The roof! firefighters started yelling. There was a shower of sparks. The roof of the Vault started to collapse. More people screamed. The roof caved in. Some of the firefighters were yelling, **Lalonde!** Other firefighters were ordering us **back, get back, get back!**

I looked behind me. Ryan the Tin Man was long gone. Scarecrow was taking more pictures with his cell phone. I wondered who in the crowd was the Cowardly Lion.

I felt like Dorothy, without the red shoes. I wanted to go home.

I didn't get a lot of sleep. I didn't bother counting sheep because I knew I'd get to ten thousand and I didn't want to spend that much time with that many sheep. Instead I got up very early. The streetlights were still on as I ran through the quiet streets. The sun was starting to come out but the birds didn't yet bother singing.

When I got to the Vault I couldn't believe my eyes. It looked like the place had been bombed. One wall wasn't much more than a pile of bricks. The police had put yellow tape around the whole building. Some really serious-looking people were poking through the rubble. I bet they were up all night, too busy for sheep.

The day after a fire is always interesting. The fire has died but it hasn't yet been buried. Sometimes you see stuff like a charred shoe or a blackened suitcase or a broken doll, but you'll never know who wore the shoe or carried the suitcase or played with the doll, and the rubble isn't about to tell you. That's why I never take pictures of fires while they're burning. No one in their right mind is going to say *What the heck?* when they see a picture of a building in flames. It is what it is. I prefer day-after pictures of fires, like my photograph of once-was-a-doll.

I didn't spend a whole lot of time in front of the building that used to be the Vault. When I looked at it, I felt like someone had punched a bunch of holes in my body. The wind went right through me and I started shivering. I decided to walk back home.

A couple of blocks later I stopped in front of a newspaper box. On the front page it said, "Flames of Fury." A picture showed these huge flames making a meal of the Vault. In smaller letters it said, "Firefighter Fights for Life." In one corner of the front-page picture was an official, stiff-looking photograph of the firefighter. I wanted to read more but I didn't have any money on me, so I stopped by a house where I saw a copy of the newspaper sitting by the front door.

The article said Steve Lalonde, the firefighter, had been gravely injured when the roof of the Goodison Building collapsed. Investigators were looking into the cause of the fire. Steve Lalonde was married and had two young kids.

Are you finished with that?

This man in a bathrobe the color of old lettuce and hair that looked like an abandoned nest stood over me. I had forgotten I was sitting in front of a stranger's door, reading a stranger's newspaper. I nodded, folded the newspaper, and gave it to him without saying a word. Nest Hair looked at me and then looked around, like he was searching for the spaceship I had landed in. I walked away.

Everybody should have a binder.

If Steve Lalonde had a binder, we would know Steve Lalonde is a heck of a lot more than what you see in a stiff pose in a newspaper. We would see photographs that tell you things about Steve that maybe even Steve doesn't know about Steve. One chapter in *Cameras and Conversations* talks about body language, which everyone speaks but not everyone understands. No one speaks in a photograph but that doesn't mean they aren't heard. What they say might surprise them. Or the photograph might reveal more than the person being photographed would want to tell.

It can take a long time for the truth to emerge, Ms. Karamath wrote to me in a letter I keep in Binder No. 1. *But one must start somewhere.*

A binder can be somewhere.

The truth is, most people aren't given a binder.

A lot of people wouldn't know what to do with it.

Some people (like Ryan) would choose to leave the binder empty.

Just because a story isn't bindered doesn't mean it won't be told.

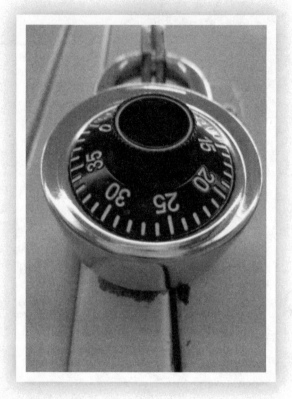

Ms. Garvey?

Some teachers call the intercom *the intercom*. One calls it *the squawk box*. Whatever you call it, it's what Mrs. Quan uses to get in touch with us during class. She's the administrative assistant for our school. Usually she says, *May I have your attention, please*, and then she tells us something that everyone in the whole school has to know about, like *This is to advise you that the second floor boys' bathroom is no longer functioning. Please use the washroom on the first floor.* No matter what she says, there's always some wiseacre who makes a comment that cracks everyone up and twists Ms. Garvey's mouth as tight as the knot in a balloon.

I know no one says "wiseacre" anymore except my grandmother and other people who are old and have dentures, but just because something isn't used a lot doesn't mean it's useless.

Ms. Garvey walked up to the intercom and pressed the button.

Yes?

Can you please send T— to the office?

As soon as I heard my name I got this hole in my stomach. Everyone turned and stared at me. The stares made the hole bigger. A couple of kids started to giggle. Mitchell whispered, **The mutant is toast.**

Ms. Garvey gave me this nod that was so small she would have needed a dozen more to make it a real nod. I got up from my seat and walked to the door. I was glad to be in the hallway, away from the whispers and stares.

When I reached the office Mrs. Quan told me to have a seat. She always looks serious and unhappy.

After about seven years Bubbles Bianco came out of his office. He looked even more serious and unhappy than Mrs. Quan.

Step into my office.

Inside his office were two police officers. One was a man who looked really young. The other one was a woman who was pretty with her hair in a bun. I should have been thinking about a lot of things, but all I could think of was that she was too pretty to be in a Diane Arbus photo.

Take a seat, T—.

Bubbles Bianco pointed to the officers.

This is Sergeant Lutz.

Sergeant Lutz gave me a nod that was almost as small as the one Ms. Garvey had given me. He had perfect hair and a perfect mustache. Sergeant Hearne didn't nod at all when Bubbles Bianco said her name. Everyone had left their happiness at the office door, if they had any happiness to begin with.

Sergeant Perfecto leaned forward. **Do you know anything about the fire on Fourteenth Street last night?**

The Vault? I unsaid. I shook my head.

We received a Crime Stoppers tip this morning saying you may know something about it.

Bubbles Bianco looked like I felt: as if he wanted to be somewhere else. **These officers would like you to open your locker for them. Can we do that now?**

I nodded.

Show us the way, then.

The two police officers followed me. Bubbles Bianco followed the two police officers. I prayed no one walking through the halls would see us. I had to go to the bathroom but I knew they would say no.

When I got to my locker, I spun the combination numbers but the lock didn't open. I tried again. Then a third time. I looked up and saw that I was at the wrong locker. Mine was next to it. When I tried my combination and it didn't click open, I checked to see that I was at the right locker. Right locker. Right combination. But something was wrong.

Relax, said Sergeant Hearne. **Take a breath.**

I didn't want to take a breath. I didn't know why the police were interested in my locker. It's a very boring locker. No mirror. No stickers. Just a bunch of photographs.

I tried the combination again. The lock released. I opened the locker.

Sergeant Perfecto told me to step aside. He pulled out my hoodie and gave the lens on the back the once-over.

This yours? Sergeant Perfecto said.

I nodded. Then he nodded. He poked around the top shelf and pulled out some books. He moved his hands around the bottom of the locker, which is a bit of a mess, with an old sweater and some crumpled-up paper. He found a pair of running shoes and gave them a quick sniff. He nodded at Sergeant Hearne, then held them up like a fisherman proud of his catch.

Are these yours?

I nodded again. He put the shoes into a bag and said they had to take the shoes down to the lab. They put the hoodie in a separate bag. The other officer told me I could close my locker and they would be in touch.

After they walked away, Bubbles Bianco put his hand on my shoulder. I didn't want his hand on my shoulder. I didn't want to be standing in the hallway like we were the last two people at an airport watching everyone else leave on a plane. I wanted to be on the plane, wherever it was going.

Do you need anything? Bubbles Bianco asked as he walked me back to Ms. Garvey's room.

I didn't know what I needed until I stepped into the classroom. It was wall-to-wall stares.

I needed my hoodie.

I went straight to Sean's house that Thursday afternoon. Sean had missed two days of school while his mother was migrained. That morning he texted that she was feeling well again but he hadn't had time to study for a test that day, so he decided to catch up at home. Ms. Karamath had been gone almost the whole week. School can feel as empty as a fishless fishbowl when your only friend and favorite teacher aren't there.

When Sean's mother opened the door, she was wearing an apron and her hands were covered with flour. **I have a lemon okra loaf in the oven**, she said. **Would you like a warm slice when it's ready?**

I thanked her and told her I was full.

Sean's mother pulled me toward the kitchen so she could give me a snack for Sean. She had arranged some figs to look like a flower, as if that would make them taste less like figs. **Sean will be happy to see you**, she said as she handed me the plate.

I wish Sean's happiness had lasted as long as the figs, which neither of us touched. As soon as I told him about the police and the hoodie and the shoes, there wasn't any happy Sean left. There wasn't much Sean at all.

You're being framed. The way Sean said it, it was a conclusion and warning wrapped together.

What do you mean? I said.

Sean didn't speak for about five weeks.

That's why they wanted your combination number. **To get your shoes. Shoes that will match the prints around the Vault.**

There are lots of shoe prints around the Vault, I said. **And why would they want my hoodie? Hoodies don't leave prints.**

Sean shrugged. **I don't know why. All I know is who. You're the "who."**

His whole face turned into a panic button before my eyes.

That's why Ryan bought you the ice cream. So you wouldn't have an alibi. You can bet he's the one who made the call.

The call?

Crime Stoppers. They want everyone to think you're the criminal who needs to be stopped. He swallowed. **You could end up in prison.**

Prison. The word pinballed in my brain. My head started to spin. We had been in the same boat for as long as I could remember. Now I was in deep water.

Boy overboard.

I don't want to go to prison.

Sean looked back at me. **I don't want you to go to prison. But —**
But what?

Sean had trouble speaking. His breathing became all short and sharp. It's like he was choking on fear.

If you tell the truth, everything's going to fall apart. I know it will. If you point a finger at them about the fire, the police will ask why they did it, and then you're pointing another finger because of Lucy.

I didn't answer. I kept thinking of one of *Lucy's Last Moments.* She's on the ground, pointing at Ryan.

Point a finger at Ryan and he'll bite it right off. He's sick. And if he gets sent away, Owen and Lee will do his dirty work for him. He'll tell them how. Sean took a deep breath. **They'll kill you, T—.**

Not before they kill you, I unsaid. I thought of *Boy Without Dog*.

Watson's gone, Sean said. **If something happens to you, I don't —**

He couldn't talk for a moment.

Please don't point any fingers. Please.

I walked over and patted his back. Before I knew it I had both arms around Sean. His arms were by his side. He kept his face buried in my shoulder. Better a lopsided hug than no hug at all.

Sean stepped back and looked at me.

I'm sorry I gave them your locker combination. I had no idea they would do what they've done.

He fell backward onto his bed. He stared straight up, as if everything he wanted to say was written on the ceiling. I looked up but all I saw was a ceiling.

What are you going to do? he finally said. I could tell the words had been sitting in his mouth for a long time.

I don't want to go to prison, I repeated. It was bad enough to be muzzled. I didn't want to be chained too.

I know.

I think I need an orange.

I could see Sean was wrong-map confused. I told him I felt like that woman in the movie he told me about, on top of the bridge, who only climbed down when the old cop offered her an orange.

I don't really need an orange. It's not about the orange, right? But then what's it about?

He shook his head. Some days I think Sean and I might have spent the rest of our lives wondering about the orange if his mother hadn't knocked on the door. She poked her head in and asked if I was having any second thoughts about the lemon okra loaf she had just taken out of the oven. I said no, and that's when Sean told her about the woman on the bridge and the cop with the orange.

What does the orange mean? he asked.

Sean's mother didn't say anything at first. She looked down at the carpet as if she was reading it. She said, **I think** — and then she paused. **I think she needed to be heard**, she said. Then she looked at the ceiling. **The orange is the policeman's way of saying he would listen.** She stepped out of Sean's room.

The woman was boatless, I unsaid. *The orange was a boat.*

I looked at Sean, but he didn't say anything else. He didn't move. I'm not sure he even blinked. It's like someone pulled a plug and all of Sean had stopped working.

I sat down on the floor at the end of his bed, next to a big basket filled with Watson's stuffed animals. I dumped them onto the floor and decided I would leave after I had put each one back into the basket. It took me twenty minutes to rebasket seven animals. A bunny Watson had chewed the bunny out of. A beakless chicken. A monkey with one ear and no tail.

They looked like I felt. Torn apart.

I don't remember walking into my house. I don't remember what I said to my parents. I went up to my room, took two photographs off my wall and one from my dresser, and laid them on my bed.

The photograph of Sean is called *Boy, Laughing*.

The photograph of Lucy is called *Punch Line*.

The third photograph was the Ryan version of *Boy with Dog*.

I took *Boy, Laughing* on a Watsonless day at the park, which was rare because if Sean was at the park Watson was almost always there too. We were at the playground, and I can't remember who said what, but one of us said something that made the other one laugh, and soon we were both laughing so hard we could barely speak. Any words we tried to squeeze in fell apart before they got through the laughter. We could barely breathe.

I looked at *Boy, Laughing*. Sean's laughter was the glue that kept me together on days when I felt like I was in a million different pieces.

The punch line was the only part of the joke Lucy could remember. That was all she needed. I can't remember what it was — something about a duck and an umbrella — but she laughed for about five minutes. She kept repeating the start of the punch line but she could never get to the end without cracking up. When she was laughed out, she sat down against a brick wall to catch her breath. She was still laughing between breaths.

Boy with Dog wasn't *Boy with Dog* anymore. It was a damaged photograph about the damage Ryan had done and the damage to come. Unless I kept *Lucy's Last Moments* to myself.

I thought of damaged Ryan. Hurting me would have been too easy. Beating me up. Taking my things. Anyone could do that. Ryan can't stand being an anyone. So he decided to kill Watson. Torture Sean. Frame me. They were holding Sean hostage and didn't need any rope or duct tape. The ransom was my silence.

I looked at *Boy, Laughing* for a long time. If I told the truth, Ryan would kill Sean. It was that simple, and that terrifying.

Then I looked at *Punch Line*. Lucy never stops laughing in the photograph but the laughter I heard was all in my head. Nothing I did would make Lucy laugh out loud again.

Ryan wanted my silence.

I decided he could have it.

For now.

For Sean.

I didn't know if Lucy would have understood or if she would have given me a hard time. I had a hunch she would have wanted *Lucy's Last Moments* to be the beginning of the end for Ryan. *Take away his flock*, she once told me between bites of a cupcake I gave her, *and he's good as naked*. She licked the cupcake wrapper clean.

But if Sean and I were a photograph, I think Lucy would have said the same thing she said about the Diane Arbus picture of the two smiling women. *They found each other.*

I had lost Lucy. I didn't want to lose Sean.

I've got something to show you.

Ryan looked up. He was sitting in a corner table in the library, reading a medical atlas. The book was open to a diagram of a heart. Maybe he was hoping to get one for Christmas.

I could see he was surprised I wasn't one of his sheep. I had waited for a moment when none of them were around. There were only a few other kids in the library that morning. Mrs. Cappel was sitting at Ms. Karamath's desk, yawning as she flipped through a magazine, looking very tired but very purple.

I sat down beside him. My heart was racing.

I promised Sean I wouldn't point fingers, I said. **That doesn't mean Lucy can't.**

Lucy's name caught Ryan's attention and didn't let go.

What the hell are you talking about?

I slid a picture in front of Ryan.

Look for yourself.

It was one of *Lucy's Last Moments*. Med and Jared are outside the frame, so all you see are Lucy and Ryan. She's on her knees, covered in baby powder. She looks really tired. One arm is raised but you can tell there's not a lot of raise left in her. She's pointing a finger at Ryan. He stands a few feet away, leaning toward her, laughing.

Ryan stared at the photograph for only a split second, but it looked like a deep split. He slid it back toward me. **I'm busy.**

He turned the page of the atlas. It was another diagram of a heart.

I nodded. **I can see that.** I placed the photograph over the right ventricle in the diagram, where he couldn't miss it.

Ryan scanned the library to see if anyone was watching. Mrs. Cappel was still working her way through the magazine. One kid used a book as a pillow.

You don't scare me. You never will.

For once Ryan and I agreed on something. You had to have feelings to be scared, and Ryan's heart was so empty I was surprised it was still working. But I had something to say and I figured *Lucy's Last Moments* was the best way to say it.

If you like the photograph, I have lots more.

I was waiting for Ryan to pounce, but he just sat there, chewing his lips. Then he said, **I thought I warned you not to play with fire.**

You did, I said. I touched my scars. **But I've played with fire and won.**

He grinned. **Right. A real champion.**

Why did you kill Watson?

I thought I saw Ryan's dead-fish eyes flicker.

Just so you know, the dog was Owen's idea. I like animals.

Because you are one, I said. The words fell out of my mouth. **You threatened to kill Sean. You torched a building that a lot of people called home.**

Ryan grinned again. **And you're the one who's going to be locked up. How do you like them apples?**

He crumpled the Lucy-pointing photograph and tossed it onto the floor.

A library is no place for litterbugs, Mrs. Cappel said. We hadn't noticed her making the rounds. She placed the crumpled Lucy and Ryan back on the table, her purple necklace swinging in his face.

I waited until she stepped away before I smoothed out the photograph and placed it back over Ryan's atlas.

If I do go to prison, and anything happens to Sean, I'm going to make sure this picture gets into the right hands.

Whose hands would that be?

Ms. Karamath.

Ryan snickered but it had no snick to it. **You're going to get a librarian to play lawyer?**

She knows right from wrong. Truth from lies.

Like it's that simple.

It's a start.

I stood up and walked away. I wasn't interested in whatever else he had to say. My heart was in my mouth but I could feel it heading back to where it belonged. As I stepped out of the library, I looked back and saw Ryan had removed the Lucy picture from the atlas. I checked the floor, looking for a crumpled ball. Nothing.

Sometimes it can be hard to shake a photograph, no matter how hard you try to shake it off.

It's nice to see you again.

Ms. Karamath was back on Monday after missing a week of school. She had a large bandage over her forehead.

Thank goodness for airbags, she said. **They had to rule out any head injuries. And they did.** She was sorting a pile of books. **A word of advice from someone who has earned it. Avoid collisions with a cement truck.**

She smiled at me. I told her it was good to see her too. I didn't tell her I wished I had seen her one Monday sooner.

Don't you have something to show me? she said. **Some photographs you thought could make a difference.**

I thought of *Lucy's Last Moments*.

I changed my mind, I said.

I'm sorry to hear that. I was looking forward to seeing them.

She picked up a library book that someone had forgotten to put on the shelving trolley.

Maybe some other time, she said.

Maybe.

You have a wonderful eye. A gift for photography I hope you keep up.

Some days I still chew on Ms. Karamath's compliment. It tastes as good now as it did then.

Bubbles Bianco stood in the doorway, waiting for Ms. Garvey to notice him. Some people who think they're important do that kind of waiting. Bubbles must have thought his importance would fill the doorway and pour into the classroom until Ms. Garvey was up to her knees in it. But she was busy with Caroline Soltau, telling her that braiding and unbraiding and rebraiding her hair was distracting to other students.

Caroline was unbraiding when Bubbles Bianco coughed. His coughs are almost as light as his bubbles but this one was loud enough for Ms. Garvey to notice. She apologized. Bubbles Bianco smiled. He took one step into the classroom.

I'm here to see T——.

As soon as he mentioned my name I felt my insides unravel like one of Caroline Soltau's braids.

Bring your things, he added.

I stood up, gathered my books and backpack, and went to the door. Bubbles Bianco didn't say anything more. He gave me this small nod, turned around, and walked toward the office. He waited for me to catch up to him. I waited for him to speak. Just when I figured there wouldn't be any bubbles, he said, **Those police officers are here to see you again.**

Tank Man, I said to myself. I had to be Tank Man–strong.

When I stepped into the principal's office, Sergeant Perfecto stood up and shook my hand. Sergeant Hearne's mouth wasn't much more than a straight line. Bubbles Bianco kept his distance, like I was contagious.

The police told me they were taking me down to the station. They told me my parents had been called and would meet me there.

A ton of words were bumper-car colliding in my head but only one made it to my mouth.

Why?

Bubbles Bianco spoke before the police could. **They're your parents. They need to be there.**

Why do you have to take me to the station?

Sergeant Hearne looked like she was about to say something but Sergeant Perfecto raised his hand slightly and spoke instead.

We'll explain everything when we're down there.

I felt bumper-car bruised and nauseous.

You won't need handcuffs, will you?

It was one of the few times I heard Mr. Bianco speak without any bubbles.

Sergeant Perfecto said I didn't need handcuffs but had to be escorted to my locker to get my jacket. Mr. Bianco asked if he could take me on his own. He made some crack about me not being **a flight risk** but the crack didn't so much as nick Perfecto and Hearne, who were all stone.

We got the jacket. Before I knew it, I was sitting in the back of a police cruiser. The drive from school to the police station felt like I was heading toward a test I hadn't studied for, in a language I was still learning.

My mother burst into tears as soon as I stepped into the police station. She was sitting beside my father. My hunch was the blame started to drip the moment she got the call. She stood up and hugged me.

I'm not surprised things turned out this way, she said.

I'm still not sure if she was blaming me or blaming herself. Maybe it was both. Some days I think there's this river between parents and their kids and you don't know if you'll ever find the bridge that connects them. Some days I think the river is bridgeless.

My mother turned to my father. He looked like his world had gotten a whole lot blacker-and-whiter. All he said was, **What next?**

I'm still not sure if he was judging me or asking the police. Maybe both.

Sergeant Perfecto asked us to follow him and Sergeant Hearne to the booking hall. I was expecting this big room with ceiling fans covered in dust. Instead, they led us into a poky room with a counter. They told my parents they had to take my fingerprints and my father nodded. I knew what to expect because of all the fingerprinting I'd seen in movies, only this was a film I didn't want to be in. I wanted to be watching it with Sean, eating buckets of popcorn soaked in butter.

After I wiped my hands clean, Sergeant Hearne led us to an interview room. On the table was a box of tissues, some bottles of water, and a folder with some papers inside. We all sat down on stiff, plastic chairs. Sergeant Perfecto pointed to a camera on the ceiling and said everything was being recorded. My father brushed his hair with the back of his hand. Maybe he thought my interrogation would go viral.

Here's what we know.

Perfecto looked at me before he continued.

We have you at the Goodison Building the night it went up in flames.

He slid a photograph across the table and said it had been taken from a security camera. It was Med, wearing my hoodie and shoes. You couldn't see his face but it had to be him. He was the only member of Ryan's crew who was the same height as me.

Is that you? my mother asked.

I didn't answer.

My father sighed a very long sigh, as if he had sprung a very slow leak.

We don't know why you did it, Sergeant Hearne said. **That's not for us to figure out.**

Perfecto nodded. **But we believe you did it. And we believe we have the evidence to prove it.** He explained how my running shoes matched footprints at the scene and that **footprints can be as good as fingerprints.**

I could see Sergeant Perfecto looking at me, waiting for my face to go from blank to billboard.

The fire started on the second floor, Sergeant Hearne said. Then she paused.

The second floor, I unrepeated. Joined at the Hip knew my hideaway was the perfect place to light a match.

Perfecto slid his chair closer to mine, as if he wanted to share a secret.

That's how it almost always begins, he said. **One match. One spark.** Another police pause. **Then things get out of control.**

Perfecto looked at Hearne. The conversation was this baton they kept passing back and forth.

We're not saying you intended to burn the whole building down. Maybe you weren't expecting a flame much bigger than a candle. A block-long pause before Hearne continued. **From what we gather, you have a thing for fires.**

A thing? I unsaid.

My mother leaned forward. **That's a terrible thing to say to a boy who —**

I could tell she was about to dish out a fresh batch of sobs. My father explained to the police officers how I got my scars.

Sergeant Hearne apologized. Sergeant Perfecto nodded and took a swig of water. Then another. Two swigs later he asked me, **Is it fair to say you like watching fires?**

I nodded.

Can you say "Yes," please? Sergeant Hearne asked.

Yes, please.

The smiles they tried to keep to themselves got away.

And that's not a crime, said Sergeant Perfecto, looking at my mother. **A lotta people gather 'round when there's a fire. But watching a fire is one thing. Starting one.** Short-as-a-toothpick pause. **That's a whole different kettle of fish.**

Sergeant Hearne leaned toward me. **Here's what I don't get. Why does a kid like you hang out in a building where homeless people sleep every night?**

I told her I didn't hang out there at night.

Perfecto told me other video footage showed me going in and out of the Vault for months.

Months? my father repeated. He sat back down in his chair, the wind knocked out of him. He took a long sip of water from a bottle.

I didn't answer. I didn't feel like telling them about the gallery, the bread box, how the Vault made me feel airbag-safe.

Then there's this. Sergeant Perfecto pulled something out of a bag. **We found it in the rubble.**

It was a camera-shaped trophy that said WORLD'S BEST SHUTTER- BUG with my name engraved beneath it. It usually sat on a bookshelf in my bedroom. Ryan must have taken it the night he broke in. The camera had been twisted out of shape by the flames.

I saw the look on my mother's face. She was as ruined as the melted trophy. My parents had given it to me for my thirteenth birth- day. I had a hunch I wouldn't be home for my fourteenth.

Is this yours? Sergeant Perfecto asked.

I nodded, then remembered to say, **Yes.**

Sergeant Hearne stood up. **You'll have a chance to explain yourself when you have your day in court. These are the condi- tions you have to read and sign before we can let you go.** She slid the papers that had been inside the folder toward me and told me that my parents had been briefed on my charges. Perfecto pointed out the court date and suggested we get a lawyer.

We have a lawyer, my father said.

My mother looked at him. **We do?**

He nodded. **Steve Ellwand.**

She shook her head. **We haven't seen him in years. And he hated my eggplant parmesan when we had them over that night. Hated it.**

I couldn't tell if she was blaming Steve Ellwand or the eggplant.

This isn't about a dinner party, my father snapped.

Sergeant Hearne sat back down and moved closer to my mother. **We'll walk you through the conditions**, she said. **You up for that?**

My mother nodded. My father pulled the papers toward him.

I had to be home from school every day at 4:00 p.m. and stay there until 8:00 a.m. the next day, when I could go back to school.

If I left the house between those hours, I had to be under parental supervision.

Same for the weekends. I couldn't go anywhere without my parents.

I was not allowed to carry matches or any other kind of material that could light a fire.

I had to report to a probation officer once every two weeks.

This all sounds reasonable, my father said. **Under the circumstances.**

He turned to my mother. She half nodded.

When he faced me he didn't try to hide his disappointment. There was too much of it to hide.

You have some explaining to do, he said.

My explanation would have only confused my parents. They would have looked at *Boy, Laughing* and *Punch Line* and that's all they would have seen. Two photographs, but not the whole story.

I was social worked by a social worker.

I was judged by a judge.

I was probationed by a probation officer.

The social worker was Call Me Sarah, the same social worker who had said ages ago that I hadn't come to terms with my scars. I spent an hour with her getting assessed. She asked me a lot of questions.

What attracts you to fires?

Tell me about this photograph.

Why the friction between you and Ryan?

I answered every one of her questions the same way: I shrugged. After every six or seven shrugs, Call Me Sarah sighed. She tried to pry me open, and every shrug was a nail. After about five thousand questions, I told her I needed to go to the bathroom.

That's fine, she said. **We'll continue when you're back.**

Okay, I said. I didn't tell her to expect more shrugs when I got back. I didn't tell her she would need a bigger crowbar.

Judge M. had one of those last names where a couple of vowels are outnumbered by a gang of consonants, so you can forget about trying to pronounce it, because when you see all those consonants standing side by side, you want to turn around and walk the other way.

I pleaded guilty to save everyone time. I couldn't bear to see the truth so twisted it could never be bent back into shape.

Roy Werker was a probation officer whose job was to write a Pre-Sentence Report for Judge M. He told me that once his PSR was completed, Judge M. would read it and decide what sentence she would give me. I asked Roy Werker what would go into the report.

You know those paint-by-number paintings you did as a kid? Dogs, clowns, what have you?

He moved his chair closer to me. We were sitting in my kitchen. My mother was in the living room.

Right now, you're a paint-by-number painting that hasn't been painted. We can see the outline but we want the full picture. Teachers. Friends. Family. They're all part of what I call the "palette." You with me?

I nodded.

You're not much of a talker, are you?

Another nod.

That's okay. Others will do the talking.

That's what I was worried about. Who would talk and what they would say. Would he speak to Bubbles Bianco? Would he speak to Ryan, who would pretend to feel sorry for how I had turned out? Mr. Ramshaw, who thought "no flow" meant "no good"? Once all the painting and numbering was done, I wasn't sure I would recognize who I was.

It would be a while before Roy Werker finished his PSR and I got my sentence, but according to Steve Ellwand, it was **a given** that I would spend some time in custody. He said I'd probably go to the Douglas Furrow Youth Center, where most people my age ended up. How long I'd stay there would be in Judge M.'s hands but it sounded like she would need more than two hands to hold it. Some days I was ready to swap all the finger-pointing tension at home for whatever was waiting for me in prison.

I spent a lot of time in my room but I never felt alone. I was there with *Woman Sweeping Sidewalk, Blind Man Feeding Pigeons, Beekeeper at Bus Stop*. I had to sort through hundreds and hundreds of photographs and choose which ones I would put on my walls at the Douglas Furrow Youth Center. I didn't know where to start because I knew how it would end: with a difficult decision. There are restrictions on what can go on the walls. It's not like I could make a floor-to-ceiling gallery. Ms. Sobetski at the DFYC told my mother I couldn't put up **more than a handful** of photographs. My mother and I argued about how many pictures I could hold in one hand. She kept insisting four was **a reasonable number**.

My reasonable four:

One of Lucy.

One without Lucy.

One that Made a Difference.

One by Diane Arbus.

The Lucy photograph was *Lucy on a Slide.*

The Lucyless photograph is *Girl with Striped Face.*

She looks imprisoned, my mother said when she noticed the photograph on my wall. *Like she's been caged.* My father said she looked like she belonged to *a tribe that worshipped zebras.*

I took the photograph in front of a face-painting booth at a spring carnival in the park. I had been there for about an hour, watching kids get turned into tigers and butterflies and Batman, when a girl walked up with an old woman who had her hair tied in a very white ponytail. The grandmother asked Melanie the face painter if her granddaughter could paint her own face. Melanie handed the girl two small jars and a paintbrush and said, *You go, girl.*

She went. She stared into the big, round rainbow mirror on Melanie's table. First she covered her face in white paint until she looked like a ghost. Then she drew these black circles around her eyes. Then she started to paint stripes down her face. After the girl finished her last stripe, she looked into the mirror for a long time. It was hard to tell if she liked what she saw but she kept looking.

I remember Lucy stared at *Girl with Striped Face* for about a week the day I showed it to her.

How old did you say she was?

I told Lucy I guessed she was twelve.

Twelve sounds right, Lucy said. She gazed at the photograph for another week. *Don't know how,* she finally said. *Don't know why. But something tells me those stripes are earned.*

Lucy turned and gently touched my scars. Then she tapped the photograph.

The way I see it, she's got her stripes and you've got your scars.

I told Lucy my scars didn't wash off.

All the more reason for you to strut. You've earned 'em.

Lucy was the first person who looked at my scars and saw stripes. Sometimes, what people say about a photograph can make a difference too.

The made a difference photograph I took with me was *Unspeakable*. The picture of the boy carrying Hector Pieterson in his arms is worth a heck of a lot more than a thousand words, and some of those words are unspeakable, which makes you listen harder to the words you do hear.

I had made copies of some Diane Arbus photographs and decided to take *A Young Man with Curlers at Home on West 20th Street, NYC, 1966*. When you first look at the photograph you can't tell right away if it's a man dressed like a woman or just an ugly woman. You can sort of see some hair around his chin but it's not like there aren't women with hairy chins. He also has long, painted fingernails and he's wearing makeup. Why would a young man want to look like an ugly woman?

You'd have to ask him, Sean said when I showed him the picture.

One of the things I've always liked about Sean is that he gives normal answers to questions about things three time zones away from normal. Most people would say Young Man with Curlers looks weird, but Sean just told me to go talk to him, as if Young Man with Curlers lived around the corner. I knew all the kids at detention would make fun of me when they saw the picture, but they were going to give me a hard time anyway, so I figured it was better to have some *What the heck?* photographs on the wall than to leave it blank.

A photograph isn't supposed to give answers. According to one photographer in *Cameras and Conversations*, it should invite questions. Diane Arbus always lets her photographs speak for themselves. She doesn't tell us if Young Man wore his curlers when he walked on West 20th Street or only wore them at home. We're never told why Child with Toy Hand Grenade is so upset.

When I'm older I'm going to go to New York City. I can tell it's a city where you can do non-normal things, like look crazy with a toy grenade or wear curlers in your hair if you're a young man. I can tell it's a city where you can live on the outside and still fit in.

46

Jared was stabbed last night.

Sean was waiting for me by the front steps at school. I could hear the shock in his voice but it wasn't just freshly squeezed shock. There was something else mixed in.

They say he lost a lot of blood but he's all stitched up and will be okay. Guess who stabbed him?

I didn't have to guess. I knew Ryan had stabbed Jared as soon as Sean told me what had happened. Jared probably thought they were in the same boat, until Ryan tossed him overboard.

Sean said he had heard a lot of things but it was all hearsay.

Jared dissed him.

Jared tried to kiss him.

Jared took a swipe at Ryan with a knife.

I chewed on all the rumors.

I feel sorry for him, I said.

Sean looked at me like I had grown another head. **Ryan?**

I shook my head. **Jared.**

You feel sorry for Jared?

I nodded. Jared wasn't as evil as Ryan. Evil was in Ryan's bones. Jared wore evil like a coat. Same with Mitchell. They were sheep that could fit into a harmless flock. Med and Lee were still figuring out if they were a wolf in sheep's clothing or a sheep dressed like a wolf. I didn't think evil was in them top-to-bottom the way it was in Ryan and Owen. I think Owen had drunk so much of the stuff he was addicted.

Sean was about to say something when Ms. Karamath walked up the stairs. She looked at me with the same heavy-eyed look as my mother. She said, **Good morning**, but the way she said it, it was more morning than good.

Sean waited until Ms. Karamath was inside the school before he continued.

That could have been you. Lying in a hospital bed. Knocking on death's door instead of Jared.

You first, I unsaid.

I pictured Jared lying in a bed, tangled up in a million tubes, with different fluids flowing in different directions.

Swing.

Sean looked at me like I had started speaking in Portuguese. I had never told him about the photograph I had shown Jared, and his reaction to it. I explained what I had done.

Maybe *Swing* was why Jared told Ryan whatever it was he told him.

Sean wasn't so sure. **You really think a photograph can do that to someone?**

I nodded. I thought of what *Boy, Laughing* had done to me.

We headed toward the front doors.

First I had to explain my plans to Roy Werker so I could leave the house without my mother.

You're trying to make good. That how I should read it?

I haven't made bad, I unsaid. I told him I wanted to honor a friend. I had a hunch he would like the word "honor," and that was the one he chewed on.

Honor, he said about fifty times. **Always in short supply. Am I right?**

I told him he was right. He said he would **shuffle some paper** and see what he could do.

After Roy Werker had done his shuffling, I spoke to Ruby. I showed her my Lucy photographs and explained that I wanted my Lucy memorial to have Ruby flowers and Ruby butterflies and Ruby birds. She smiled and stepped into her parents' Half-a-Block-from-the-Corner Store. A few minutes later she stepped out, holding her mother's hand. I could see Mr. Lam watching through the window. He had so much mistrust in his eyes I was surprised it wasn't running down his cheeks.

Ruby's mother was about half the size of Ruby. She smiled at me and kept smiling as Ruby spoke to her and pointed at me. Some pointing is fully loaded but Ruby's finger was empty. I had never heard Ruby talk so much. Her excitement was this sauce that covered her shyness. Sometimes she said a word in English. Once in a while Mrs. Lam would ask a question and Ruby would look at me and then give an answer, and Mrs. Lam must have liked what she heard because she kept smiling.

She says it's okay, Ruby said. Then the sauce was gone, the shyness returned, and her mother went back into the store.

One of Lucy's favorite poles was about five blocks away from the Lams' store. She would put her crate against one side of the pole and lean her signs against another. Then she would stretch her legs out on the sidewalk and close her eyes. Sometimes she hummed. Sometimes she napped. After about fifteen minutes she'd wake up, rattle her coffee cup, and go back to being Lucy.

I covered the pole in my favorite photographs of her and added a crate at the bottom.

Ruby sat down on the sidewalk and carefully placed a small bucket of chalk beside her. She stared at the Lucy pole for a long time. She was so still you could forget she was only about ten years old. I don't think Ruby was ever her age. I had a feeling she was ten by the time she was three.

Then she started drawing and didn't stop. She started with a sunflower and ended with a Ruby meadow.

Her work was beautiful, but I knew it wouldn't last. It would get stepped on and fade and get washed away by the rain. The Lucy pole would go back to being just a pole after the Lucy photographs were

torn off or covered with flyers for garage sales or missing dogs. It wasn't the tombstone she deserved. But I couldn't bolt a milk crate to the sidewalk. I couldn't build a fence around the pole. The best tombstone for Lucy would have been in a cemetery with rows and rows of marble tombstones, and one made of cardboard with black-marker letters that said *Please Wait to Be Seated*.

One woman stopped and looked. First at Ruby's drawing, then at Lucy.

I know her! she said. **That's . . . That's . . .**

Lucy, I said.

The woman put down a big briefcase. She had her hair in a bun with a pencil going through it.

Is that her name?

I nodded.

Where is she?

Dead, I unsaid.

Instead, I said, **She's gone.**

The woman pulled the pencil out of her bun and started to chew on it.

She had the funniest signs, the woman said. **You know what you should do?** She didn't wait for me to answer. **You should publish them. In a book. All of her signs. You could make a fortune. I mean, funny sells, right? "Will pole dance for food." I loved that one.**

She laughed and looked down at the sidewalk as if Lucy was still there. It looked like she was thinking about Lucy, even if she was remembering a different Lucy than the Lucy I knew. She smiled as she looked at all the different Lucys displayed on the pole.

She was such a character, the woman said. **Too bad she's gone.**
She picked up her briefcase and walked away.

I wish she had taken the word "gone" with her. It stuck to me as soon as I heard her say it. I could tell the empty feeling that came with "gone" wasn't going anywhere soon. I thought of Lucy's last moments. Was there someone who had pictures of Lucy's first moments and middle moments and some of the million moments in between?

Then Jared showed up.

His arm was in a sling. The rumors were that Ryan might have killed him if the knife was a few inches longer. There were a thousand different versions of what had happened that night.

The day after the assault, Ryan's parents put him in a private school. Maybe they were hoping things would smooth over, but Jared's parents had other plans. Ryan was charged and awaiting trial.

Jared stood there, as stiff and still as the pole. He raised his slingless arm as if he was about to touch *Bouquet*, then changed his mind. He looked as gray as the sidewalk beneath Ruby's drawing.

Who invited you to the party? Owen shouted from down the block.

I saw Ruby go from shy to scared as Owen, Med, and Lee approached. Owen's voice was like a bell that woke up the Jared who had once been Joined at the Hip. He suddenly looked at me like I had an L-for-Loser on my forehead as permanent as my scars but Owen wasn't buying it.

Did you hear me? he said to Jared. **Who invited you to the dipstick's party?**

I did, I lied. **And it's not a party. It's a memorial.**

A memorial, Lee repeated, looking at Ruby's meadow.

That's not all of it, I said. I had been standing in front of the Lucy pole. I stepped aside.

Oh, Jesus, Med said. I could see he wasn't expecting to see that much Lucy in one spot.

Not Jesus, I said. **Lucy.**

Owen stepped toward me and leaned in. **Trying to be funny?**

No. I leaned back. **Truthful.**

Owen looked at Med and Lee. He must have figured it was his moment to lead the flock now that Ryan was out of the picture. He raised his foot over a bird as if he was about to smother it. Ruby's body shrunk into itself.

Don't, Jared said. He grabbed Owen by the arm.

Back off, Owen said.

Jared motioned toward Ruby. **Her father will be all over you.**

Like I'm afraid of her father? he sneered. **Don't tell me what to do.** He turned to face Med and Lee. **Let's get outta here.**

As they walked away, Jared looked at the pole one last time, then headed in the other direction.

Hey, I called out to Jared. He turned around. **Thanks.**

I could see he wasn't expecting that. I don't know what he told Ryan that night. In my head Jared showed him *Swing* and said something Ryan needed to hear. But Ryan doesn't discuss. He destroys.

Now I had given Jared what he deserved, and that was the problem. He was having trouble pretending it was wrong to have done right.

He walked off and didn't look back.

I turned to Ruby. **Are you okay?**

Her **Yes** was feather-soft.

I have to take you home.

I looked up at the sky and was relieved. All the clouds were mashed-potato white.

Two days later a heavy storm washed the meadow away. Most of the photographs were torn off the pole but I didn't mind. I liked the idea of pictures of Lucy being tossed and scattered by the wind, landing on Lucyless streets and yards and making them Lucyful.

I didn't even bother trying to read Judge M's face. It wasn't just a closed book; the title was in a language so foreign I wasn't sure it was still a language. Plus you would have to skip to the end of the book to get to my sentence, because I knew she was going to spend pages and pages talking about me and *this whole sorry mess.*

My mother was sniffling like there was no tomorrow, and if there was a tomorrow she wouldn't have noticed because she was too busy sniffling. It doesn't happen often, but my father looked uncertain, like he was at a funeral without a casket.

I knew the judge had read my presentence report.

What did you tell Roy Werker? I had asked Sean.

The truth. How you're not someone who would torch a building. How you don't have a mean bone in your body. How liking fires and starting them are two different things.

I'd told Sean I bet that added lots of color to the portrait Roy Werker had painted of me. Sean said he wasn't sure because Roy Werker told him that **good friends don't make for good juries.**

He had been chewing on a straw. **I'm not glad you're being sent away.** He pulled the straw out of his mouth and stared ahead. **But I'm glad you'll be safe.**

You would have done the same for me, I had said.

I felt bad for him. I was going to take a bullet so he could dodge it, but he had no clue he was the dodger. I knew Sean and I would always be best friends but things wouldn't be the same as long as I hung on to what I knew he didn't know. *Same* had been booted out and *different* had moved in, and once *different* moves in, *same* is never allowed back, no matter how long it stands at the doorway.

When I faced Judge M. I had that same won't-get-past-the-doorway feeling. She talked about how it was important to put everything in context. Then she spent so much time putting things in context that I didn't think we would ever get out. She spoke about my good marks in school. She described how some teachers thought I was **diligent**. She mentioned that others described me as **anti-social**, which is what happens when you stick to yourself because people like Joined at the Hip are always sticking it to you. She wondered if I had **an unhealthy preoccupation** with fires because I was often seen at them.

Then she spent about six weeks asking if the **trauma of a childhood accident can lead to unforeseen consequences**, including **unpredictable behavior**. She talked about the destruction of the Vault, how Steve Lalonde was on a very long road to a full recovery and might not walk again. Finally she got to my sentence.

Seven months in custody and a hundred hours of community service.

My mother's sniffs burst into an unpluggable wail. My uncertain father suddenly looked like he was certain I had it coming. Sean looked at me. He didn't have to say or unsay anything. I knew he'd be there when I got out, waiting in our boat.

My so-called funeral was two months ago. If I was dead, that means I'd be in heaven and where I'm living sure as heck isn't heaven. It's just me in my room at the Douglas Furrow Youth Center. Me and Lucy and *Girl with Stripes* and Hector Pieterson and *A Young Man with Curlers*.

There are rules about how many photographs you can stick on the walls but no one said anything about a shoe box beneath my bed. That's where I keep a bunch more.

The morning before I left for Douglas Furrow, Sean asked if he could have a copy of one of my pictures to give to Mr. Lam.

In *Girl Holding Chalk*, Ruby looks up at the sky as if she's deciding where to add a cloud. Sean thought the photograph might **soften Mr. Lam up**. The way he described it, Mr. Lam grunted and looked at the picture like he was seeing a Ruby he had never seen before. A few grunts later he put it by the jellybean jar next to the cash register. The next day it was in a frame.

When my parents come to visit they always have the same how-did-we-end-up-here look. It's like they pulled into a train station on a boat. They're still trying to figure things out but so am I. There's a lounge where we sit and talk, but the truth is we do more sitting than talking. That's when my father brings out the Scrabble game. The first time we played, my mother came up with a great word: OXEN. I looked at my tiles and wished I had the letters to spell LUCY. I pictured a Scrabble board filled with some of the words that had been swimming in my head. ORANGE. UNSPEAKABLE. STRIPES.

I wondered what my parents would think of all my tiled words. I wondered about all the words they've kept inside, words that were swallowed instead of spoken. I pictured all our inside words as tiles on the table. We were a small family but we would need a bigger table.

Two weeks after I got here I received a package from Ms. Karamath. It contained a blue binder, a yellow one, and a green one, each filled with blank paper. There was a sticky note on each binder. The blue binder is to *paint a picture of the difficult journey* leading up to where I am today, Ms. Karamath said. As if I had run out of food and water, gotten sunstroke, and traveled on a half-blind mule to get here.

The yellow binder is to describe the seven months at Douglas Furrow.

The green one is for the one hundred hours of community service.

I opened the blue binder. Inside was an envelope. Inside the envelope was a letter from Ms. Karamath.

Though I have been teaching for more than fifteen years, it behooves me to keep learning.

I knew there would be a lot of head-scratching words like "behooves" in this letter. Ms. Karamath is like that. She would rather give you a *What the heck?* word to chew on all day than a word you can't even taste.

I am trying to understand how a fine young man like yourself could have wrought such damage. A firefighter's life will never be the same. A building is now little more than rubble. You were found responsible and are being held accountable.

"Accountable" is a word that's served a lot here. It gets about as much attention from most kids as the once-were-vegetables that are tossed onto every plate at lunch and then tossed out.

I can't explain your actions. Nor am I asking you to justify what cannot be justified. But I do know that in all the discussions that have been raging — in classrooms, in the cafeteria, amongst my colleagues — your voice has yet to be heard.

I don't know what a raging discussion looks like but I wouldn't want to get too close to one.

I believe you owe it to yourself and your parents and those who care for you to share your story. I suspect your insights will illuminate. Despite all that has happened, I know you to be curious and compassionate, a loyal friend and a gifted photographer. It can take a long time for the truth to emerge. But one must start somewhere. And so I give you these three binders to fill with your artful photographs and your considered words.

I'm two photographs away from finishing the blue binder.

He has a real name but everyone calls him Slice because that's what he wants to be called. No one is going to argue with him because if you did he would take your argument and crush it with one fist and hand it back to you in pieces. Slice says about five words a day, so when he speaks everyone at Douglas Furrow listens.

He told me he liked my photographs. He didn't say it right away. He just looked through my shoe box like he was shuffling through a deck of cards. Sometimes he stopped shuffling and stared at a picture the way Lucy did when I showed her the Diane Arbus book. Like the picture was talking to him. I could tell Slice was listening but I wasn't going to ask him what the picture was saying. It's not like his nickname is Hug.

After all the shuffling and staring, Slice stopped at one picture I call *Young Man with Bent Spoon*. He looked at it for about six years before he said anything.

Gonna keep this.

I nodded.

He kept staring at the picture as he walked off, followed by a string bean sidekick who was more side than kick.

I took *Young Man with Bent Spoon* one day as I was walking up to Sean's apartment. The Young Man was hanging out, staring at someone or something I couldn't see. You look at the photograph and you wonder if he was given a bent spoon, or if he was given a

normal spoon and he bent it. And if he did bend it, you wonder why. Or if he'll unbend it. You can stare at the photograph all you like and you won't get any paint-by-number answers. Maybe that's why Slice liked it. Maybe he feels as misunderstood as some photographs.

You Slice's new squeeze?

I didn't hear Ryan approach. Snakes don't make a heck of a lot of noise.

No, I said.

Ryan arrived at Douglas Furrow about a month after I did. He was found guilty of assault and sentenced to five months. He'd been trying to raise a flock but hadn't gotten very far.

I forgot, Ryan said as he put his hand on my shoulder, like we were old friends. **You and Sean are like this.**

He crossed two fingers. **Even after what he did to you.**

He uncrossed his fingers. **Hanging you out to dry.**

I knew what Ryan was trying to do. He was prodding me the way I once saw Joined at the Hip poke at a squirrel trapped in a trash can.

Some friend.

I stared at Ryan. **What do you know about friendship?**

There's a fifth photograph I added to my wall. No one has said it's one too many. It arrived a few days after I got here.

You can't see the dog tag in Sean's other hand.

I wondered if Med and Lee and Owen and Mitchell would be waiting for Ryan when he got out. They stuffed their faces with lies but I don't think they knew what loyalty tasted like. They were driven by fear, and Ryan did all the driving.

When are you going to take my picture? he said.

I looked at Ryan. **I already have. Remember?**

He grinned but I could tell it wasn't a real grin.

I showed it to you that day in the library, I said. **Lucy's pointing. You're laughing.**

Ryan looked around but Little Bo Peep had lost all his sheep. He stepped forward, staring at my scars. His half grin was dangling on his face.

I looked straight at him. I didn't move. I felt like Tank Man.

Ryan was going to say something but the words fizzled before they ever popped.

I walked away.

Halfway across the yard I smiled.

I remembered a photograph of a rusted tank that some torn-shirt kids were swinging on. The tank had been stripped clean of its tank-ness and turned into a playground. The war that had been warred was over. The kids were from some country where they had to dance around land mines or they would never dance again. But in the picture they're smiling singular smiles.

AUTHOR'S NOTE

Diane Arbus created unforgettable portraits of people who lived on the fringes of society. She started as a fashion photographer, but over time, she migrated toward such offbeat settings as cheap hotels and circus sideshows, where she found people who left her feeling "a mixture of shame and awe." These contradictory push-pull feelings help explain the power that fuels Arbus's work. Her most memorable images are both magnets and mirrors: They draw our attention and remind us that our differences make us human. She doesn't provide any easy answers, but challenges us to reflect on what we think we see and who we really are.

Arbus is widely considered one of the greatest photographers of her generation, but those who scale the heights of acclaim often find themselves tethered to controversy. On the one hand, Arbus broke barriers by placing the eccentric front and center. But some critics believe she used the dwarf, the giant, the tattooed man to her advantage, sidestepping their dignity as she furthered her career. She died in 1971, at the age of forty-eight. Years after she walked off the beaten path, after she stepped into the neglected corners where differences thrive, her work continues to be exhibited around the world.

For all the unique traits revealed in an Arbus photograph, there is a universal quality to her portraits. "My parents had divorced and there was a general feeling of loneliness, a sense of being abandoned," Colin Wood explained in a 2005 interview. He was the child holding the toy hand grenade in Central Park in 1962. "I was just exploding . . . She captured the loneliness of everyone."

The photographs mentioned in this book, in order of appearance:

Masked Woman in a Wheelchair, PA, 1970

A Jewish Giant at Home with His Parents in the Bronx, NY, 1970

Mexican Dwarf in His Hotel Room, NYC, 1970

Child with Toy Hand Grenade in Central Park, NYC, 1962

Untitled (1), 1970–1971 [two women wearing flowered hats]

Puerto Rican Woman with a Beauty Mark, NYC, 1965

King and Queen of a Senior Citizens Dance, NYC, 1970

A Young Man with Curlers at Home on West 20th Street, NYC, 1966

Behind every iconic photograph stood a photographer who was there, camera in hand, to capture a moment that, indeed, made a difference.

Sam Nzima was in Soweto, South Africa, in 1976, when Mbuyisa Makhubo carried Hector Pieterson in his arms, with Hector's sister Antoinette Sithole by his side. More than one hundred and seventy-five people died during the Soweto Uprising, which marked a major turning point in the country's long struggle with apartheid.

The harsh truth about napalm is forever linked to a harrowing photograph of Phan Thị Kim Phúc running down a road near Trang

Bang, South Vietnam, in 1972. Immediately after Nick Ut (born Huỳnh Công Út) snapped the picture for the Associated Press, he took Kim Phúc to the hospital. He won the 1973 Pulitzer Prize for the photograph, officially titled *The Terror of War*, and he is still in touch with Kim Phúc, who now lives in Canada.

Jeff Widener created an indelible image of the single individual, who became known as Tank Man, holding shopping bags as he faced down a convoy of tanks in Beijing, China, during the 1989 Tiananmen Square protests. Tank Man's identity and fate remain unknown.

ACKNOWLEDGMENTS

A bit of sleight-of-hand happens when a book is published. An author's name goes on the front cover but that doesn't tell the whole story. There are several gifted, generous people who helped make this *Young Man*. To craft a novel with Cheryl Klein, executive editor at Arthur A. Levine Books, is to see every word handled with the care and consideration it deserves. I am deeply grateful to Cheryl for insights that turned ideas inside out, for a rigor that enriches, for her lifelong passion for children's literature. The seasoned hands of Anne Shone, senior editor at Scholastic Canada, deftly shaped all aspects of this book from the moment the manuscript landed on her desk. Anne's grace, instincts, and commitment set the stage for all that followed. By her side was Erin Haggett, the tireless assistant editor who offered a steady stream of input and coordinated the photo shoots with endless goodwill. Art director Christopher Stengel artfully choreographed the cover, and the dance between words and images. Thankfully there's no need to shout from mountaintops with a story to tell when you have the devoted, wheels-keep-turning marketing team of Bess Braswell and Emily Morrow (New York) and Denise Anderson and Nikole Kritikos (Toronto) in your corner as publicist Jennifer Abbots beats a drum on your behalf. Ann Behar's timing was spot-on when she stepped in and offered representation. Thank you to Arthur A. Levine for his blessing and to Diane Kerner for her support. To copyeditor Elizabeth Starr Mayo and the rest of the production team at Scholastic, I can say without a drop of false modesty that I couldn't have done this without you.

David Wyman rarely steps out his door without a pocket-sized camera. Lucky us. A handful of the striking photographs he has taken on his strolls have taken this novel to a different plane. His portraits haven't simply lifted the characters off the page; they are their own stories. I was blessed to have Maria Vacratsis, a wonderful actor, tell us so much as Lucy without saying a word, and I am indebted to all the troupers who helped stage this fictional world: Max (Sean); Claire-Marie (Ruby); Sam (Boy Holding Purse); Leonie (Girl with Goldfish); Alex (Young Man with Bent Spoon); Amanda (Girl with Striped Face); and Trudy Weiss (Woman with Painted Eyebrows). Jarred left his mark on the cover even though you don't see much more than his hand. Two dogs — Tuco (Watson) and Roman (Mr. Jackson), not to mention a goldfish — brought life to this story as only animals can. Lisa Chambers, Liz Dingman, and Joy Mason offered much-appreciated behind-the-scenes support. Nora Church and Jax Remark transformed Maria into Lucy thanks to their skills, respectively, as a makeup artist and hair stylist. Simon Kwan, graphic designer at Scholastic Canada, transformed a sidewalk into a meadow for the Ruby photographs. Emily Chan, a lawyer at Justice for Children and Youth, ensured I got things right when things went wrong for T—. The mark Diane Arbus left on this story is as singular as her photographs.

Generous financial support from the Toronto Arts Council and the Ontario Arts Council fell like sweet rain on the long journey that is novel writing. My big-hearted mother, Olga, sprinkled some of her own. Leave it to young readers to offer the unvarnished truths a writer needs to hear: Thanks to Michelle Gram for recruiting some of her students, and to Findley Dunn, Collin Dang, and Tamara

Goddard (and her mother, Anne Francis, who read it aloud) for their thoughts on early drafts of the manuscript. And while Toby, an incorrigible Westie, makes Watson seem well-behaved, our daily walks fuel me.

Ten years passed between the moment I first gave thought to this story and the day it became a hold-in-your-hand book. During that time my two daughters, Sophie and Molly, went from lively young girls to lovely young women, embroidering my days with untold joy. My wife, Kathy, is my sea and shore. They are but three, yet they are everything.

ABOUT THE AUTHOR

Emil Sher writes for the young and the once-were-young. His works for children include board books, picture books, a ballet, and Breadbox Theatre, which he created to introduce early-grade students to live drama. He is the author of *Mittens to Share*, illustrated by Irene Luxbacher. Emil's original plays, which have been performed internationally and translated into Hebrew, Italian, and Slovak, include *Sanctuary, Bluenose, Beneath the Banyan Tree*, and *Mourning Dove*. He has written stage adaptations of *Hana's Suitcase*, the beloved Holocaust story by Karen Levine, and Ian Brown's *The Boy in the Moon*. His feature-length screenplay, *Café Olé*, was honored with a Canadian Screenwriting Award. Emil has been a playwright-in-residence at several theaters, his fiction and nonfiction have been widely anthologized, and his radio plays have been broadcast around the world. He lives in Toronto with his family and a dog that ignores him on command. For more information, please visit emilsher.com.

ABOUT THE PHOTOGRAPHER

David Wyman is a professional graphic designer as well as a freelance photographer. His creative work has received numerous international honors, including the Canadian Library Association Award for the Advancement of Intellectual Freedom in Canada. He lives in Toronto. To see more of his pictures, please visit his website at www.wymandesign.ca/PHOTOS.html.

This book was edited by Cheryl Klein
of Arthur A. Levine Books and
Anne Shone of Scholastic Canada,
and designed by Christopher Stengel.
The production was supervised by
Elizabeth Krych. The text was
set in Adobe Garamond, with a
hand-lettered title treatment.